STOCKING STUFFERS

A So Over the Holidays Novella

ERIN MCLELLAN

"I loved Stocking Stuffers! The sexual tension sizzled from start to finish. McLellan weaves sex toys, experimentation and curiosity perfectly into the intimate moments between Sasha and Perry ... Get this book as a gift to yourself for the holidays!"

—Rachel Kramer Bussel, editor of Best Women's Erotica of the Year Series

"Steamy, snowed-in fun with a fabulous, sex-positive heroine and a smitten, blushing hero who will make romance readers swoon. Grab the tinsel and the toys because Stocking Stuffers will put you in a festive, sexy mood!"

—Layla Reyne, RITA Finalist and bestselling author of Dine With Me and the Fog City Trilogy

"With a Scrooge-like heroine who owns her sexuality with a boldness that is admirable and refreshing, and a sensitive hero who's a lover of romance books and family, Stocking Stuffers is a fun, kinky and yes, swoony, holiday romance packed with laughs, hot sex, emotion and a love that will have you rooting for the happily ever after in ugly Christmas sweaters. I absolutely loved it!"

—Naima Simone, USA Today bestselling author

Sasha Holiday is so over the holidays after getting left at the altar last Christmas Eve. But as the marketing maven for Lady Robin's Intimate Implements, she's stuck not-so-merrily pitching naughty toys at a romance book club's Christmas party. Her loathing of the yuletide only intensifies as a snowstorm rolls in and traps her at the Winterberry Inn. Stranded with her is Perry Winters—a hot bearded book club member trimmed in flannel and tattoos.

Perry's a romantic with an unerring belief in the magic of the season, and he recognizes a Christmas miracle when he sees it. Brave, smart, and confident—Sasha Holiday is a gift. And the gifts keep coming when she suggests they pass the time with some no-strings fun. After all, she has a big bag of toys that would make even Santa want to stay in bed on Christmas Eve.

But the frisky festivities turn complicated as feelings spark between Sasha and Perry. Perry wants to see Sasha once the snow clears, but Sasha is reluctant to take the relationship sleigh ride again. Perry will have to show her that love is more than just a holiday feeling.

Chapter One

Sasha lifted the toy from her huge red bag with a flourish, and the jingle bells on her reindeer antlers tinkled merrily.

"This little darling, the Love Bite, is my favorite of the bunch." She displayed the toy in her hands like a model on *The Price is Right*. She'd found, after years of peddling her wares to anyone and everyone who would listen, that drama sells. Especially at Christmas. "The handle is ergonomic, and it's sturdy. Frankly, there is nothing I hate more than a flimsy sex toy."

The Staunchly Raunchy Book Club members tittered, and Sasha grinned. "Y'all know what I mean. I can tell."

Gently teasing the clients was one of Sasha's customer service tricks. She was adept at figuring out which Lady Robin's Intimate Implements partygoers were gregarious and bantering with them. But today, Sasha's heart wasn't exactly full of holiday cheer *or* consumerism. She felt like the fake elf at the party, and she'd never been a very good faker.

"The Love Bite uses suction technology, and I swear to the Ghost of Good Orgasms Past, it's the closest to real oral I've ever found in a sex toy. You just place the head over your clit and it creates a suck-and-release sensation," she said matter-of-factly.

Sasha normally loved filling in at a Lady Robin's sales party when one of the regular reps called in sick. She loved chatting with the clients, and she definitely loved the commission money.

But she *hated* Christmas, so this party sucked.

Sasha passed the Love Bite to Valerie, the party's hostess and a beautiful femme lesbian, who tested the suction on her thumb.

"Oh, very nice," Valerie said. "I might give up the girlfriend search for this baby." She waved the Love Bite at her friends. "This is my new girlfriend now!"

Sasha couldn't hold in her professional pride. "Plus, it's waterproof."

Sasha's friend, Robin, had started Lady Robin's Intimate Implements, a boutique sex toy and lingerie company, as a pop-up shop seven years ago. Sasha had been the whole of the marketing department for the first three years before their company had exploded into a multi-city operation. They supplemented their online and local vendor sales with bridal showers and birthday parties attended by their salaried marketing reps. This was the first book club they'd been commissioned for, as far as Sasha knew. Their company had made Robin, and Sasha by extension, stockings full of cash.

A blast of wind hit the Winterberry Inn, causing the old house to creak and rattle. Sasha whipped around to see out the big bay window. It was dark out there, and she desperately hoped the expected snow and ice held off until she was home. Her darling baby—a restored 1984 VW Bug—was a disaster on icy roads.

Valerie, who owned the Winterberry Inn and was definitely the evil mastermind of the Staunchly Raunchy Book Club, called a pause on the proceedings to get everyone mulled wine and spiked eggnog. Sasha took the brief reprieve to glance around the luxurious hearth room. The inn was a cozy bed and breakfast with seemingly endless rooms and Christmas charm in every nook and cranny.

The hearth room spilled over with Christmas bobbles, garland, boxwood wreaths, and lights. A huge spruce tree, decked out in glittery gold, was activating Sasha's allergies.

Christmas made her itch, even when it was beautiful.

Maybe especially when it was beautiful.

Once the book club members were back in their circle of seats, Sasha pulled a paddle out of her bag and pasted on a fake smile.

"We don't have a huge variety of impact-play instruments, like crops or whips, but if you're in the market for that, I can give you suggestions for other vendors. We only have one paddle, but it's exceptional, if I do say so myself." She brandished the wooden paddle Robin had

3

created for the holidays. It had a word etched into the wide, flat end. "You can personalize the word, so it could be your name or your partner's name. Other common words are *BABY* or *SLUT*. This is our Christmas edition, you know, if Santa gets you going."

The group laughed as she handed off the paddle adorned with the word *HO!* The book club members had been discussing a BDSM romance novel when she'd arrived, and the group erupted in chatter as they deliberated over whether the characters in the book would have enjoyed such play.

Sounded like they definitely would have been down.

Sasha listened to them with half an ear as she removed the last items from her bag. For a perverse second, she wished her roller bag was velvet, like Santa's, rather than boring nylon. Velvet would match the red dress she'd donned in the hopes of appearing to be a bundle of cheer.

False cheer, but whatever.

Once the room quieted down, Sasha displayed her final toys.

"Last but not least, next month we're debuting a new line called Prick Me, for the person or persons in your life with dicks and prostates, but we have a bit of stock available for purchase today. Call it a sexy sneak peek."

She waved one of the toys—a holly-green cylinder with an opening on one end. "Here is our Fancy Flesh-stroker, which comes in twelve diverse skin tones and several fun colors. These have a soft, silky interior and are super easy to clean. We're also debuting two vibrating prostate massagers of differing shapes, named, quite simply, the P-Spot Pulse and Pulse 2."

She held them up and demonstrated how to turn them both on.

A quiet, earnest-looking white woman named Louise laughed. "This might sound stupid, but can you explain how those work?"

Sasha smiled, a real one this time, and put her proverbial sex-educator cap on. "So the prostate is a gland in front of the rectum in people born with penises and prostates. It has tons of pleasure sensors, so it can feel good when it's stimulated. A lot of people with prostates enjoy having theirs touched, and that isn't specific to certain sexualities. Prostate play can result in some pretty spectacular orgasms. With consent, of course, all you have to do is lube this baby up and insert it into—"

A big *thump* resounded almost directly behind her, and she dropped the toys onto the hardwood floor. Somehow, the vibrator on the Pulse 2 was activated on impact, so it buzzed and danced all over the place.

As she scrambled down to grab the toy, trying not to flash everyone since her holiday dress was *short*, Valerie shouted, "Perry! What are you doing here?"

Sasha got the toy turned off before twisting around. There was a man standing in the entryway of the room, a gym bag—evidently full of bricks considering the noise it had made when hitting the ground—by his feet.

Hot damn.

He was the type of man who could make her Christmas knickers twist. Tall, lean, pale, with dark curly hair and a beard. Plus, he was staring at her like she was a piece of rum cake.

She wanted to be his rum cake.

Double damn.

He ran a hand roughly through his hair. "I drove in a day early to beat the winter storm, which didn't work. It's already icy out there. I didn't expect to walk in on my favorite book club getting a sex-toy demo." He didn't take his eyes off Sasha.

Chuckles filled the room, and Sasha slowly stood up. No one seemed particularly perturbed about being interrupted by this man. Instead, the room was alight with excitement at his arrival. She smoothed her red velvet dress down with one hand while clutching the sex toys in the other. Her stupid antlers jingled.

Valerie waved an arm dismissively. "Well, you showed up a day early, so …"

"So?" He was still staring at Sasha, his gaze tracking over her face.

"So maybe it's your own fault if your delicate constitution can't handle talk of prostate massagers," Sasha said with an extra dose of sass.

A grin slowly spread across his face, and dear God, he was hotter than she'd realized.

"Fair assessment. I'm sorry, we've never met. I'm Perry Winters." He finally drew his attention away from her and checked out the members of the Staunchly Raunchy Book Club. "I think I know all the other Raunchies here, but not you."

Raunchies? Was that what they called themselves? Because that was adorable.

He stuck his hand out, and Sasha stumbled on her way over to shake it. His hand was sturdy and huge. Occasionally, Sasha loved the feel of soft, delicate hands, but Perry was making her crave large, strong, and callused.

"Sasha, and I'm just the sex-toy marketeer."

His eyes darkened deliciously at that. "I doubt you're *just* anything."

"Perry's my brother," Valerie said. "He used to be in our book club before he moved to Topeka, like a dweeb."

His hand began to slip from Sasha's, and she jerked her palm from his. They'd held on too long. "You were in *this* book club?" she asked. He was one of the Raunchies?

"Yes. I like to read," he said, as if it were that simple.

Which, really, *it was.*

"That's awesome," she said. *And sexy.* She kept that part to herself.

"Hey Perry, have you read the newest Minnesota Motorcycle Club book?" asked Andie, a petite black woman. She was wearing an ugly Christmas sweater with kittens on the front and had slapped a nametag on her chest that said, *Holiday Pussy.* Sasha wanted to be her best friend.

Perry smiled warmly. "I haven't. I DNF'ed the last one, but maybe I'll give the new one a shot," he said.

Most of that went over Sasha's head, so she returned to her seat and sat primly, waiting for the group to calm down again. After the excitement of Perry's arrival wore off, Sasha looked to Valerie to see if she could continue.

"Right! Sorry, Sasha. We'll let you wrap up, then we'll dive into our game of Dirty Book Dirty Santa."

"Sounds good." Sasha eyed Perry, who'd pulled a folding chair into the circle and was watching her, unconcerned.

It wouldn't be the first time she'd hand-sold sex toys to men, but he made her skin prickle. Made her feel squirmy and excited all at once.

She cleared her throat. "As I was saying, here are our prostate massagers. Use lube."

She directed that last comment at Perry. Rosiness rushed up his cheeks above the line of his beard as he smiled. A blusher. Mayday, too cute for words!

Without stopping to swoon, she continued, "I've also got a catalog for lingerie and underthings that you're welcome to peruse. Our lingerie is size and gender inclusive with a select range of bras, garters, slips, undies, binders, compression gaffs, and strap-on bottoms, all with Lady Robin's rock-and-roll flair. Now, does anyone have any questions?"

Louise raised her hand timidly.

"Yes?"

Louise bit her lip and glanced at Perry. He was a former Raunchy, so they were probably used to him being present, but Louise was obviously not comfortable asking this question in front of him.

Perry stood up abruptly. "Oh man, that eggnog smells amazing. I'll be back." He rushed toward the breakfast room where the food and drinks were set up. With a smile, Sasha watched his long legs and tight ass waltz from the room.

He was a blusher *and* considerate of women's feelings. She wanted a bite.

Once he was gone, Louise laughed. "Gosh, sorry. I couldn't ask this in front of him. Do you have anything in double-F sizing?"

"Definitely. Everything, including our bralettes."

A few other book club members had questions about sizing and prices as well. As Sasha answered, another huge gust of wind made the house shudder and the lights flicker. She needed to hurry so she could get home before the roads were too treacherous for her Bug.

"Here are the order forms. I have some stock with me today, but if I don't have what you want, we guarantee its arrival in five business days anywhere in the continental US. Feel free to check out the items on display. If no one has any questions, I'm going to run to the restroom real quick."

Valerie directed Sasha to the closest bathroom in a hallway off the huge, gorgeous kitchen, which was also decorated with all manner of garland and Christmas candles. There was a centerpiece made of a grapevine wreath, red garden roses, and berries on the kitchen island. Sasha stopped and stared at it, her heartbeat in her throat.

It was eerily similar to the centerpieces she'd made a year ago for her wedding, only a lot fancier. Like a gut punch, it halted her in her tracks. Blood suddenly thundered in her ears, and her stomach pitched, a metallic taste hitting the back of her tongue. She had to squelch the urge to swipe the centerpiece off the counter and hurried out of the room instead.

Once Sasha was alone in the hallway, she leaned against the wall and tried to slow the frantic patter of her heartbeat. Her phone buzzed in her hand, which was more effective in distracting her than the deep breathing.

It was a weather alert. They were in a Blizzard Warning.

Fucking great.

She also had a text message from her older sister, Rosie.

Rosie: *Roads are horrible on the west side of city. Hope you're not out being wild.*

Sasha: *I'm wrapping up a Lady Robin's party. Will leave soon.*

Rosie was a worrier and a pessimist. Sasha was sure their little brother, Benji, had received a similar message.

Rosie: *Who the hell plans a sex toy party right before X-mas? You need to get home now!*

A laugh worked its way out of Sasha's throat, surprising her.

Sasha: *The dirtiest and coolest book club ever, that's who. Sex toys make the best stocking stuffers.*

Rosie: *Very funny.*

Sasha: *I am. I'll text when I leave. This place is out in the boonies, so I have at least an hour drive to get home.*

It wasn't really the boonies. There were plenty of

other properties around, but to a city girl like Sasha, it might as well have been the great frontier.

"Sasha?"

She jumped at Perry's deep voice and bobbled her phone until it slithered through her fingers and skittered across the floor. Thank God for super-protective cases.

"*Baby Jesus!* Stop making me drop things."

"Sorry. I didn't mean to startle you."

He swooped down and picked up her cell phone. Their fingers brushed when he handed it back, and she shivered. He smelled of cedar.

She liked it. A lot.

Maybe he was a lumberjack. He *was* wearing flannel.

He smiled, his eyes bright. "I feel like I crashed your sales pitch. I'm sorry if I made it awkward."

"Don't worry. I'm not shy."

His gaze landed on her lips before jerking away. "I think half the book club is heading out soon, and the rest are staying at the inn to wait out the storm. They're drawing names for a book exchange rather than playing Dirty Santa."

"Oh, that's good. I'll go get their orders, so I can head home too."

He took a deep breath. "This might be out of line but would you go to dinner with me sometime this week?"

Her pulse galloped off like a herd of reindeer. She hadn't been on a *date* date in ages. Dates led to expectations and crossed boundaries. She hadn't dated since ... well, since the worst Christmas ever had soured the idea of relationships for her forever. Being left at the altar on Christmas Eve did that to you.

Rather than spill her issues on an unsuspecting hot guy, she said, "A date? All you know about me is that I sell sex toys for a living."

Some people thought that made her available or even a slut.

"No. I know you're smart and confident, and I like your voice. There's this lilt when you speak, like you're always having a great time and everything is funny. And your hair. I like your hair."

"Wow. Thank you."

A few of her regular lovers had not been fans of her hair when she'd chopped it into a pixie cut a few months ago. Needless to say, they weren't her lovers anymore.

He ran an unsteady hand across his chin and lips. In the darkness of the hallway, she couldn't see his eyes clearly. She wondered what color they were, wanted to see them alight with pleasure. She had a feeling Perry would be delightfully expressive and genuine in bed.

"I'm not the best at this," he said, voice shaky.

"You're actually doing pretty awesome."

"Really?"

"Yeah, really, but I'm not the dating type. And regardless, don't you live in Topeka?"

His smile withered, and she had the irrational urge to cup his cheek.

What was happening to her?

She wanted to blame her sudden soppy, sweet feelings on the Christmas cheer in the air. It was like those parasitic spores that latched onto everything, multiplied, then smothered their host.

"I *did* live in Topeka. I, uh, I'm not … My living situation is complicated."

"I'm not in the market for complicated," she said. "Though, you're super cute, so I'd probably be game for a night together. A one-night stand, basically. But not tonight because, you know, snow and ice and rear-wheel drive. I need to get home."

His mouth had gone a little slack, and she inwardly cringed. She tended to steamroll people. Men especially expected her to be more circumspect about her sexual appetites and romantic boundaries, but that wasn't her problem. It was theirs.

"I'm sorry. I can't tell if you're rejecting me or propositioning me," he finally said. The corners of his eyes crinkled.

"Both."

"I like you," he said decisively, and she laughed.

"I'm a bit much, I've been told. I like to fuck, eat, masturbate, and read, and I don't do any of those in moderation. Still interested?"

She had no idea why she was unleashing all her sass on him. Maybe to scare him off. Or to see if he'd stick around.

"I'm definitely still interested, Sasha."

"Then here's my number." She rattled it off for him, and he hurriedly input it into his cell.

They smiled at each other like two dorky teenagers before the sound of someone humming a Christmas carol in the kitchen jolted them apart.

"I'll be out in a second to wrap up everyone's orders. I need to hit the road before the Bug can't make it up the driveway," she said.

"I wondered whose car that was."

"My baby brother restored it for me a couple years ago. He's a little genius." She grinned just thinking about her brother, who at six foot four was in no way little or a baby.

"It's beautiful."

"I know." She winked and slipped into the bathroom.

The partiers were almost done drawing names for their romance novel exchange when she returned, so Sasha prepared to fill and file their orders.

Once they wrapped up, she clapped her hands once. "Okay, Staunchly Raunchy Book Club, does anyone have questions? I'm ready to take your orders if you have any."

A stack of order forms were passed in her direction. Her payout for this party would be a nice holiday bonus. Maybe she'd take her siblings out to their favorite Chinese restaurant on Christmas Day.

It took her about ten minutes to distribute the stock she had with her, accept payments, fill out receipts, and file the remaining orders. By the time she'd sold her last Love Bite, the wind was howling and whipping snow against the huge windows of the hearth room.

She didn't even have an ice scraper in her car. Her grandmother was probably rolling in her grave over how unprepared Sasha was for bad weather.

"Thank you for doing this," Valerie said with a solemnity that might have been due to too much mulled wine.

Louise nodded and bit her lip. "I've wanted to try out a vibrator, but I've been too self-conscious to go into a shop, and I wasn't sure how to pick one online. Some of the companies look sketchy."

"That's why I love this job. We want to make it easier and more comfortable for people to find and purchase what they want and need," Sasha said, dropping her voice to give the three of them privacy. "Sex toys are fun, and they're essential for some people, particularly women, to get off. There's nothing shameful or wrong about that. Technology is a wonderful thing."

"*Exactly*," Louise whispered, tucking her long, frizzy brown hair behind her ears. "We read so many sex-positive romance novels where the heroines have all this sexual agency, but here I am—too chickenshit to buy a vibrator. Well, no more. I bought two."

"Good." Sasha grinned at her and made a mental note to include a couple of coupons with Louise and Valerie's orders. "I'm happy you scheduled Lady Robin's for your holiday party. This was such a fun group."

"You're welcome to join the book club! We're always excited to indoctrinate unsuspecting humans into our romance novel cult," Valerie pitched in.

"Thank you, but I'm not exactly local. I live on the far side of the city, over an hour away, but I'd love book recommendations. I enjoy thrillers, so maybe romantic suspense? I'll give you my email."

Valerie whooped and rushed off to get a pen and

paper. Sasha smiled in her wake. Valerie was beautiful, especially now, when she was flushed, uninhibited, and excited about books. Perry and Valerie both had dark curly hair and killer smiles. They could have been twins. But there was something about Perry, something that hit her right in the chest.

What was that exactly? Chemistry, maybe? Lust? Sometimes she was knocked over by it, by that rush of adrenaline and discomfort, when she wanted someone. When the thrumming in her pulse spiked from, *Oh, I like their smile*, to, *Oh, I want to sit on their face*. But this dose of Perry felt exceptionally potent.

Gender had never factored into it for her. She liked women. She liked men. And she liked people who were both or neither or fluid. But regardless of gender, she had a type.

Unexpected. Adventurous. Expressive. Emotional.

She had no idea if Perry had any or all those characteristics, but she couldn't help but hope he'd call her eventually so she could find out.

Valerie rushed back over with a notepad and pen as Sasha finished packing up her bag of unsold toys. Sasha was writing out her email address for Valerie when Perry materialized beside them.

Sasha, of course, jumped at his sudden appearance and dropped the fucking pen. He picked it up for her.

"Dray is giving a bunch of people a ride home since they have that huge minivan with the all-wheel drive. Andie and Karen are hoping to stay here until the storm clears if you have space," Perry told Valerie.

"We have enough rooms," Valerie said.

"Do you have space for me too?" Louise asked.

"Absolutely." Valerie winked at Louise, which made her blush. Then Valerie turned to Sasha. "Will you be able to make it home? You could stay here. We always have room at this inn."

"Oh, uh. No, I better not." Sasha glanced at Perry. It was tempting, but she didn't think she could survive the Christmas extravaganza going on at this place for longer than a few more minutes. "I appreciate the offer, though."

"Of course," Valerie said. "Thanks again for coming. I think I've officially hosted the best Staunchly Raunchy Book Club Christmas Party ever."

"Yeah, those toys will make awesome stocking stuffers," Perry said.

"That's what I said!" Sasha exclaimed. "Batteries not included, though." Perry tipped his head back and laughed, his whole face transforming, opening up with humor and happiness. And oh man, she loved a good laugh. She had to wrench her gaze away from him before she was caught staring. "I'm going to brave the weather and head out."

Valerie, amazingly, gave her a hug before she hurried away to see the other guests off. An unusual emotion lumped in Sasha's throat at the two seconds of friendly contact. She wasn't much of a hugger. Her grandma had been the bearer of hugs in the family, and maybe she and her siblings had been working at a deficit, because a platonic hug from a stranger at Christmas shouldn't have made her want to bawl.

Perry's voice brought her out of her navel gazing. "It's bad out there. You sure you'll be okay?" He was watching her closely. Now she could see that he had hazel eyes, an intriguing mix of green and brown. The lights from the Christmas tree reflected in them like stars.

"I'll be fine."

"All right. I'll walk you out."

She donned her coat and trudged out into the snow, pulling her two roller bags of sex toys—lighter than when she'd first arrived—behind her.

The snow was mixed with pelting ice. The door handle on her VW Bug was so cold it burned her hand when she opened it. Perry helped her load the bags.

A solid coating of ice covered the back window, but it wasn't as thick on the sides and front. She turned the car on and flipped the heater to defrost.

"I don't have an ice scraper," she said, embarrassed. She was a strong, capable, independent woman, and it sucked to be caught unprepared. She parked in a parking garage at her apartment and at work, so her car wasn't sitting out in the elements very often.

"I think I have two. Hold on." He rushed over to a hulking silver SUV and pulled one long-handled and one smaller scraper out of the backseat. He handed her the bigger one, then without a word, started in on the back window.

She attacked the ice on the front window with a vengeance, taking out her frustration, sexual and other-wise. She was seriously regretting the red velvet dress, thigh-high fishnets, and black stilettos. This was the worst winter-weather outfit ever, and her coat wasn't doing much to cut the cold.

They finished quickly, which was great, since Sasha was freezing her snowballs off.

Perry took a step closer to her. He had snow frosting his dark curls and beard.

"I don't feel good about this. The weather is atrocious," he said.

"I'll be fine," she repeated, glancing up the huge hill she'd have to drive to make it out of the Winterberry Inn's driveway. It was an ice rink. If ice rinks had a twelve percent grade. This was a horrible idea.

"I'm going to text you, so you have my number. Will you call if you have any issues getting home?" Perry asked.

"Sure. It was nice to meet you, Perry. I hope you text me sometime but, you know, not just because of a little winter weather."

"Oh, I plan to." He swooped in and kissed her briefly on the cheek, barely a touch. But his lips were warm against her chilled skin, and it sent a shimmery arc of heat through her. She shivered, and he must have misinterpreted it, because he opened her driver's side door, and said, "Get in before you catch a chill."

Catch a chill? She was mouthing those words to herself, a small smile flirting on the edges of her mouth, as she put the car into gear. What an old-fashioned phrase. Perry waved at her, and her smile grew. She started the steep climb up the driveway.

Maybe Perry was really into those historical romances

her sister enjoyed—the ones with dukes and scandals and carriage rides. She could almost see him as a brooding Regency hero, except his smile was too unrestrained.

Next she imagined him shirtless and in a clench with a woman in a beautiful fancy dress, because why not? It was such a pleasant fantasy that the first skid of her baby's tires came as a total surprise.

Adrenaline exploded in her gut like a pipe bomb.

She was suddenly too hot, and the sticky, bitter taste of fear burst on her tongue.

What if her car's traction wasn't good enough to get up the hill? Her engine was a dinosaur. She was a month late on changing the oil because she was obviously irresponsible.

Then her Bug shuddered, the tires stopped spinning, and the car slipped backward.

Chapter Two

$\mathcal{P}$erry watched as Sasha's clunker chugged up the driveway. He was concerned her car wouldn't make it up the hill. As kids, he and Valerie had raced skateboards down that slope, seeing how fast they could go, the wind whipping against their faces until it was like they were flying. Surely, old ass Volkswagen Bugs were not built to climb icy, Midwestern hills.

His eyes had adjusted to the darkness, helped along by the Christmas lights flashing from the eaves of the inn and the snow blanketing the ground. Sasha surprisingly made it most of the way up the hill with no problem, and he was about to go back inside, when her taillights abruptly pitched to the right, then slid backward.

"Shit," he said under his breath, panic shooting his heart into his throat.

Her VW Bug slipped all the way down the hill before her brakes reengaged and she came to an abrupt stop.

She pushed her door open, and he rushed over. Her

jaw was tight, her delicate mouth pinched. But it was her eyes that alarmed him. The blue of her irises was nearly invisible—her eyes much too dilated, even for the darkness.

He crouched down next to her. "Sasha. Are you hurt?"

"What? No. I didn't hit anything. The ice just made my car slide. I think I need more power to make it out."

He grimaced. The problem with this driveway was that there was no room to build up the momentum she needed, especially in the ice. His family had gotten snowed in here for that very reason at least five times that he could remember; though, it had never happened to him as an adult.

"I'm going to try again in a lower gear," she said. Her hands were shaking on the steering wheel, probably from adrenaline. He wanted to rub them, still them, but he suspected she wouldn't appreciate that right now.

"Okay."

"Stand back. If I slide down, I don't want to hit you."

"Sure thing." He stepped farther into the yard and the rapidly accumulating snow. Visibility was getting worse. The thought of her driving home in this weather hurt his stomach.

She accelerated up the hill but only made it about halfway before her wheels locked up, then spun out again, flinging snow and ice everywhere. This time she managed to stop on the hill and not slide down, but she couldn't budge. She eventually reversed back down the slope and rolled down her window.

"Fuck."

"Yeah," he said. "I think Val has some kitty litter I could try spreading at that steepest bit, see if it gives you the traction you need."

"Yes please, Mr. Winters."

After finding half a bag in the lean-to garden shed, he climbed up the hill until he reached the problem area and scattered the gravelly kitty litter. With a wave of his arm, he indicated she should try to drive up again.

The ice and snow mixture was hitting him square in the face, obscuring his vision and soaking him through. His teeth chattered as the Bug started up the hill.

No dice.

The car skidded to the right and the wheels spun out. Sasha quickly wrangled the car back under control and guided it down the driveway. She reached the bottom of the hill as Valerie walked out of the front of the inn and waved. The snow was falling harder now, almost whiteout conditions, making it hard to see.

Sasha climbed out of her car as he made his way to her, her bright red skirt and green coat a homing beacon to him through the blizzard.

"I'm screwed," she said as she pulled out her phone. "I wonder if an Uber could meet me at the top of the driveway. Fuck, that will be expensive. I live so far away, and then I'd be without my car on the other side of the city."

Her hands were shaking, and Perry didn't know if it was adrenaline or the cold.

23

He lightly touched her elbow. "I could drive you home." He did have a big SUV, after all.

Val obviously didn't like that idea. She shook her head immediately. "Too dangerous. Conditions are deteriorating too fast for anyone to be on the road. Not you, not Sasha, not an Uber driver."

Sasha let out a long, gut-wrenching sigh. "Yeah. Shit."

"You can stay here," Perry said. "I'm sure there's an open room, isn't there, Val? And if not, I could always sleep on the couch in the carriage house."

Val nodded, seeming to think out loud. "Louise can stay in the extra room of the carriage house with me, and the love birds will be in the Jack Pine Room."

"Who are the love birds?" Sasha asked.

"Karen and Andie. They're newlyweds. Let's see," Valerie said. "The Boltons left a day early to miss the storm, so the Blue Spruce Room is open. We can put you there, Sasha, on the house of course, hon. Perry, I planned to give you the Red Cedar Room since it's your favorite."

Excitement rushed through Perry. In the Red Cedar Room, he'd only be separated by an en suite from Sasha. Which, actually, she might not be crazy about.

"We'd be sharing a bathroom," he told Sasha, so she wouldn't be surprised.

Her eyes got big. "Cozy."

"Hey," he whispered, trying to cut Valerie, his nosy sister, out of the conversation. "If that makes you uncomfortable, I understand. I can sleep on Valerie's sofa."

"*Pshh.* It's fine, hot stuff. Told you I wasn't shy." This

time Sasha reached for his arm, placing a reassuring hand on him. He couldn't help but lean into her touch, and she watched his face without wavering, a flash of heat in her eyes.

Valerie cackled. "Okay, *that* tension is thick as fruit-cake, just saying!"

Perry closed his eyes and prayed for the icy ground to open up and swallow him whole. Sometimes older sisters sucked.

Sasha snorted a laugh before stomping her feet, like she was trying to keep warm. Her shoes were shiny black pumps, and his brain split in two trying to decide if he loved the way they made her legs appear miles long or if he was worried about her toes and frostbite.

She must have followed his gaze, because she said, "Inappropriate footwear. Name of my memoir."

"They look nice, at least." They looked more than nice. *Sexy.*

"Cold, though."

"I bet."

"What do you think? You okay staying here until the blizzard passes?" he asked.

"That could be days, right? Wasn't that the forecast? It wasn't supposed to hit until tomorrow morning, though."

"Weathermen are crooks," Perry said with a smile. "Let's get you inside. You're trembling." He retrieved her sex-toy bags, which scrambled his brain a bit with lust, before they walked inside together.

"I don't have any extra clothes. Or a toothbrush." She

lifted an unsteady hand to her forehead. "I'm sorry. I feel so unprepared."

"Oh, don't worry about it. I'll loan you some comfy stuff," Valerie said. "And we have any type of toiletry you'll need. Lucky you got snowed in at a bed and breakfast. Hospitality is kind of my thing."

Perry and Valerie led Sasha up the stairs to the Blue Spruce Room. When he opened the door for her, she stumbled back into him.

"Yikes."

He peeked around her to see what had spooked her, but nothing was out of the ordinary.

"What's wrong?" Valerie asked.

Sasha seemed to shake it off. "Oh, nothing. Wasn't expecting it to be so … seasonal, that's all."

Valerie and Perry glanced at each other and laughed. Winterberry Inn had been in their family for three generations. It was *known* for its Christmas charm. During the other seasons, Valerie toned it down, but winter was in their blood, literally.

"You can blame our grandfather for that," Perry said. "He set the precedent of a Christmas tree in every room back when party lines and rotary phones were a thing."

Valerie squeezed Sasha's shoulders gently. "I'm going to go grab you pajamas. Perry can show you around in the meantime."

"Cool, cool, cool," Sasha whispered under her breath. She rolled her bags into the Blue Spruce Room. "Ah, Christmas lights on the four-post bed. Neat. And berry swag around the window—okie dokie. I see there are glittery pinecones on my bedside table. That's … something."

"Oh my God. You hate Christmas!" Perry leaned against the doorjamb and grinned.

"I do not!" She whipped around and stared at him. "Okay. That's a lie. I despise it. And it's like Christmas afterbirth in this place."

"Gross."

"I agree."

They smiled at each other before Perry had to shake himself. He could stare at her all night. She was gorgeous.

And also only interested in sex, which was not usually his cup of tea.

Wait. That came out wrong. He wasn't bad at sex.

Correction—he didn't *think* he was bad at sex. He'd never had complaints. He'd never had a one-night stand either and wasn't sure if he'd excel in that arena. In fact, his recent career and love-life shakeups had made him doubt himself in more ways than one.

"Let me give you that tour." He offered her his elbow.

She rolled her eyes and her grin widened, finally seeming to relax a little. Then she shucked off her green trench coat and threw it on top of the plaid bedspread.

"Lead the way, Mr. Winters."

"Gladly, Miss …?"

"Holiday."

"Ah, festive."

"Shut up." She tucked her hand into his elbow, a pleasant, warm pressure, and he led her out of the room.

"This whole hallway is guest rooms, as are the ones a floor up. I'm here."

He pointed to his door as they passed it. They walked down the staircase, which was adorned with balsam fir garland and tasteful white twinkle lights. He loved the smell of the house at Christmas, loved the mix of greenery and lights and warmth.

Nostalgia from his childhood hit him in the chest. He'd missed this. Maybe coming home after his career had fallen apart in Topeka had been the right decision after all. A fresh start was exactly what he needed.

When they reached the foyer, he pointed to the basket of blankets. "If you want to sit on the front porch, feel free to take a blanket from here. I can't imagine that'd be fun in the blizzard, though."

They walked into the formal sitting room. This was his least favorite room. It was stuffy, even when covered in Christmas. Next was the breakfast room, which still had refreshments from the Staunchly Raunchy Book Club party.

"This is where Val and her chef serve breakfast every morning. But you can come in here anytime. There's always baked goods."

He picked up a leftover chocolate éclair, but as he moved it to his mouth, Sasha grabbed his hand and directed it to her mouth instead. His breath caught and his eyes were drawn to her lips as they wrapped around the pastry. She took a bite, never breaking eye contact.

"*Fuck*," he hissed, his whole body firing with lust.

"What do we have here?" a woman said from the doorway, humor in her voice.

Andie Romero—biggest troublemaker in all the land. She was wearing a Christmas sweater with cats on it.

Perry closed his eyes, sad about the interruption, and Sasha turned away from them both, choking on a laugh, her mouth full.

Karen Romero, Andie's wife, waltzed up next to Andie. Karen was a middle-aged, five-foot-nothing FBI intelligence analyst, who could command a room with nothing more than an arched brow. Perry wished he had her presence.

"They were canoodling," Andie whispered.

"Were not," Perry said like a five-year-old. He wished they'd been canoodling.

Sasha managed to swallow her mouthful of éclair around her laughter before turning back toward the women. "Perry was very kindly showing me around, considering I'm stranded here."

"At least you're in the best of company," Karen said, teasingly tossing her locs over her shoulder.

"Thank you, Karen." Perry was touched she'd say that.

"I mean *us*." Karen grinned at Sasha. "Come on. We'll show you where the stingy Winters keep the wine."

"It's called a wine cellar. Not exactly a secret," Perry said.

"Yeah, but most guests don't get the security code. We're special. Karen interrogated it out of Valerie," Andie said. "Follow us, kiddos. Bring your éclair."

Karen and Andie led them through the breakfast room into the hearth room. The fire had died down to glowing embers, making it cozy and warm. The Romeros didn't stop to admire the charm. They grabbed Sasha's hands and dragged her through the formal dining room —all decked out with boxwood wreaths, winterberries, and unlit candles—to the laundry room and the cellar door.

"The code is 1225," Karen said. "Christmas."

"Cute," Sasha said. She reached back for the éclair Perry was holding, and he handed it over. She grinned.

The wine cellar wasn't anything special, but the Romeros gasped in excitement and started talking a mile a minute.

"What type of wine do you like?" Perry asked Sasha, while their chaperones were distracted.

She shrugged and ran her finger over a dusty bottle. "Cheap and red. Maybe boxed."

"Oh dear," he said. "That will not do at all."

"Are you a wine snob?" She lowered her voice. "I refuse to sleep with a wine snob."

He pressed a hand to his chest. "I'm not a snob. I have taste. There's a difference." Though being newly unemployed had made his wine obsession a bit compli-cated, but that was what was wonderful about having a sister with a well-stocked cellar.

Andie appeared in front of them, a grin lighting up her expressive face. She was wearing black lipstick and looked like a total badass. "Hey, wine snob. You choose.

You'll know what's too expensive. We don't want to piss your sister off when we filch it."

He watched as Sasha finished her chocolate éclair, her lips wrapping around the luscious dessert. He knew just the thing. Humming, he stepped over to the short, squatty bottles of port and late harvest zins.

The 2013 Venge Vineyard Late Harvest Zinfandel. *Perfect.*

Karen strolled over and nicked it from his hands. "A dessert wine when only one of us has had dessert." She threw a glance over her shoulder at Sasha. "How fitting."

"Let's go back upstairs and have dessert, then, ladies." Perry tried to send Karen his most winning smile, hoping to charm his favorite FBI analyst.

After a long beat of side-eye, Karen said, "I like where your mind's at, kid."

She took Andie by the hand, still holding the wine bottle, and directed them out of the cellar.

They reached the hearth room. Someone had set it back to rights from the Staunchly Raunchy Book Club, so there was no longer a circle of chairs. It was once again a cozy sitting area with the wood-burning fireplace as the centerpiece.

"Why don't you all sit," he said. "I'll get us wine glasses and the desserts."

"I'll help," Sasha said.

Perry gathered up four wine glasses and a corkscrew, and Sasha grabbed the platter of leftover desserts and a stack of small plates. There were chocolate éclairs, apple tarts, slices of German chocolate cake, chocolate-covered cherries, and lemon bars.

"God, who made all this? It looks amazing," Sasha said.

"Probably Valerie. The inn has a chef, Eden, but Valerie was a pastry chef before taking over here, and she likes to flex those baking muscles every once in a while. Plus, the chocolate cake is our mother's recipe."

They slipped back into the hearth room and were met with quite the romantic display. Andie and Karen had cuddled up on a loveseat and were whispering with their heads together. Karen laughed at something Andie said in her ear, a secret, soft laugh that was completely at odds with her usual toughness. Then she lifted Andie's fingers to her lips to kiss her knuckles.

"Sweet," Perry said quietly.

Sasha smiled, but it was almost pained. Sad. "Yep. Very."

"Oh, there you two are! Bring us the corkscrew, slow-poke," Andie called to Perry from across the room.

Sasha dished out their desserts for them. Perry opened the wine and poured everyone generous helpings. He grabbed an éclair—Sasha had eaten his earlier—and settled down into a large, comfy wingback chair next to the fire. Sasha selected a few chocolate-covered cherries and a piece of German chocolate cake.

Perry couldn't take his eyes off of her as she took her first bite of cake. She hummed happily, watching the fire-place, then took a sip of wine. The deep red of the wine against the berry-color of her lips made him dizzy and hot. He wanted her to love the wine. He wanted her to love the cake.

Hell, he just didn't want her to be incredibly upset about being stuck here at his family's legacy. Here with him.

She moaned. "Shit, this is good."

Karen and Andie agreed, eating their desserts with relish.

They all sat in comfortable silence. A log rolled in the fireplace and split apart, causing crackles and a slight flare of flames. Karen pulled out her phone and fiddled with it for a few seconds. Then Christmas music floated from its speakers. A Bing Crosby classic.

Perry smiled. There was a blizzard outside, and his whole life was packed into cardboard boxes in the back of his SUV, and he hadn't told his sister that he'd lost his job, but this—this right here, with Sasha and the Romeros and Bing Crosby—was perfection.

Sasha stood abruptly, like her cushy armchair was on fire. "I need to go."

"Are you okay?" Perry started to stand, but she waved him down. She finished the rest of her wine in a couple gulps, which *scandalized* him.

"I should call my sister, let her know what happened. She'll be worried." She held up the empty dessert plate and wine glass, as if she'd forgotten they were in her hands. "Uh, I'll go put these—"

"I'll take them." Perry gently removed them from her hold. "No worries."

She nodded stiffly. "Thank you." Then she was out of the room, her velvet dress swinging around her thighs.

"Someone's allergic to Christmas music," Karen quipped dryly. "Doesn't take FBI training to see that."

"She needs a little holiday loving, I bet," Andie added.

Perry snorted. "Busybodies." But he couldn't stop watching the doorway Sasha had left through. What if she was freaked out about being here? What could he do to ease her mind, make her comfortable?

Karen snapped her fingers at him. "Loverboy, go find her. Make sure she's okay." She lowered her voice. "Get laid."

He shook his head. "No, I'll help you two clean up and—"

"We'll do it," Andie piped in. "Anyway, we want to make out, and you're killing the mood."

Now it was his turn to stand like his seat was on fire. "Fair enough."

He didn't actually think he'd find Sasha, especially if she'd retreated to her room, but he didn't want to cramp Karen and Andie's style. Both of them had demanding jobs—Karen a FBI analyst and Andie a bartender and PhD student—so maybe they were using their snowed-in status as an excuse for a romantic getaway.

This was a wonderful place for that. In fact, the inn was renowned for the romantic Winterberry Christmas Couples' Soiree, but he'd never brought a woman to it. It was hard to be romantic at a B and B run by his own sister. As he reached the second-floor landing, movement in a nearby sitting room caught his eye. He peeked through the doorway. The room had no fewer than four small Christmas trees tucked into every available space, and in the corner, there was an old upright piano that was permanently out of key. These trees were strung with red wooden beads and threaded popcorn. A model train set circled the largest pine.

Sasha was as still as an ice sculpture in front of the large window. She'd pulled aside the curtains, and the reflections of the Christmas lights in the glass cast a warm glow around her head, like a halo.

"Snow's getting worse," she said, without glancing back at him.

"Seems like it."

"My sister said the news is calling it a snow-pocalypse. They always say that though, don't they? Hope they're exaggerating. I could be stranded here for days, if not."

"That wouldn't be so bad, would it? At the very least, there will be awesome desserts."

She turned to him. He sat on the piano bench, facing her.

"There might be other perks as well," she said softly, her eyes assessing.

"Oh yeah?"

"Yep." She took a few steps until she was standing right in front of his legs.

He had to tip his head back to see her face. Their closeness, the sudden heat between their bodies, his exposed throat—it made his breath catch and hitch with longing. She ran a light fingertip over his Adam's apple, and he swallowed thickly.

"Follow me, Perry." She strode from the room, and he did what any person with half a brain would. He obeyed.

He caught up with her at the door to the Blue Spruce Room, where she grabbed his hand and pulled him inside but didn't close the door behind them.

She let go of his hand and knelt in front of the red roller bags she'd deposited at the foot of her bed. What in the world was she doing?

She bent down and fiddled for a second before reappearing in front of him.

"Uh, thanks for helping me try to get up the hill today and for showing me around. And for the wine and chocolate. You're very nice."

"I'm pretty sure I wasn't that helpful."

"Still. You got wet and cold, and now you'll probably catch that chill." She pulled a long, rectangular box from behind her back. "Here. Take this. On the house. As thanks."

"Oh, you don't need to do that. You don't owe me anything," he said but instinctually took the box when she handed it over.

She backed away and zipped up her bag, not looking at him.

"Did you just give me a sex toy?"

After a beat, she said, "A super nice one, yeah. It's our sparkly gold version. I wish I'd gifted it more smoothly, but I don't regret it."

He glanced up and laughed. "Fancy Fleshstroker."

"Stop chuckling and accept this inappropriate token

of my appreciation. Merry Christmas to you," she snarked, and he laughed harder.

"I've never used a sex toy. I'm not sure I'd know what to do with this."

"It's not exactly rocket science. It's about as handy as, well, your hand."

"Are … gizmos like this necessary, though?"

A sharp grin spread across her face. She was absolutely beautiful.

"Gizmos? You're asking the woman who is the head of marketing for a successful sex-toy company if she thinks they're necessary?"

Oh, she was out of his league. "I'm sorry. I didn't mean to offend."

"You didn't. But to answer your question—no, they're not *always* necessary. Sometimes they're simply fun. I bet you'd have fun with that." She gestured to the box in his hand. "Toys can increase pleasure or spice up sex. Some people with clits can't come without vibration. How necessary are sex toys to them? I'd say pretty essential. Have you heard of the orgasm gap?"

"Yeah."

"One of my goals—one of the goals of Lady Robin's Intimate Implements—is to show that it doesn't have to be that way. People with clits can have as many orgasms as people with dicks. Sex toys can help a person discover what they like, what they don't, what they need, how their partners can please them, and how they can please themselves. We strive to empower our customers, of all genders, to take control of their sexual pleasure. That's why my friend Robin started the company, and why I wanted onboard."

It was as if she'd hit him over the head with a bag of coal. He'd felt the same way when he'd walked into the hearth room earlier and seen her standing there in front of the Raunchies with a prostate massager in her hand. Sasha was a good salesperson—professional, passionate, confident—and it turned him on to an inappropriate degree. Turned him on enough to ignore the fact that he normally wasn't at all interested in one-night stands but would happily fall at her feet for one.

"I have to admit, I really enjoy listening to you talk about sex toys," he said.

A hush fell between them, thick with tension.

"So," she said. "Relationships are not my cup of eggnog."

"Yeah, I remember."

"But here we are, snowed in, and I have a big red bag of toys ..."

"And I could be your willing student?"

"You have no idea how much I want to teach you some things."

"I'd love that." He took a deep breath. "I've never done this, though." It felt like there was a flock of turtledoves roosting in his stomach.

"Sex?"

"With a stranger."

"Well, lucky you, because I'm an awesome stranger, not a sucky one. And we don't have to do anything you don't want to do." She glanced toward the doorway on the far side of the room. "Does that lead to the en suite bathroom we share?"

"Yes. It's only accessible from our rooms, not the hallway."

"Oh, convenient. Come with me." She headed toward the bathroom, tugging one of her roller bags behind her. "Bring the Fleshstroker!" she called.

When he finally picked his tongue up off the floor and trailed her into the bathroom, locking the door behind him, he couldn't do much besides stare. She'd long-since ditched the reindeer antlers, and her silky, dark-blonde hair shone in the lights of the bathroom. Her hair was perfectly *her*. Sweet and edgy at the same time. So short that it drew focus to her big blue eyes and adorably pointy chin.

She also had curves galore, with an ass that made him want to worship her.

Plus, she was washing a black dildo in the pedestal sink. It was obviously new because the packaging was littered around the vanity.

With a grin over her shoulder, she said, "Hand me the Fleshstroker."

He tore into the box and passed it over. She washed and dried the internal sleeve quickly. The whole process surprised him. He hadn't expected the Fleshstroker to have removable pieces, and he probably wouldn't have thought to clean it before use. She loaded batteries into the black toy, and it sprang to life in her hand before she clicked the vibrator off.

The lights in the bathroom were too bright, and the

overhead fan drowned out his panting. He loved this bathroom. It was retro, with white and navy tile, a claw-foot tub, and a modern shower. He checked to make sure the door leading into his room was locked as well.

He had no idea what was about to happen, but he was in. He was her faithful student.

He was hers.

For tonight, he belonged to her.

"You still with me?" she whispered, sidling closer.

"I want to kiss you so badly I can hardly breathe." The words blurted out of him, like he had no control over his own mouth.

"Oh, good answer."

Then her lips were right there, right under his. The electricity of that first touch weakened his knees. Weakened him but made him feel stronger too.

Her fingers immediately tangled in his hair, and he had to shut down a groan. It had been too long since someone had touched him like it was integral to be skin to skin, lips to lips. And oh, damn, her lips. They were soft and sweet, and she kissed him with absolutely no reservations or timidity. She went for it. All in, like she was hungry for his lips and tongue and teeth. Their kiss lit up his whole body.

He skimmed his fingertips across the back of her neck and down the long line of her spine. His hands ached to clutch and cup and manhandle.

"Grab my ass," she whispered against his lips, as if she'd read his mind. "I don't want polite."

Well, *hell*. He could try impolite for once. He snuck his

hands down to her thighs and rucked her pretty red dress up around her waist. Then he grabbed her bare butt, his thumbs skimming the top of her satiny thong. God, she felt amazing.

"What do you want?" he said in her ear, causing her to shiver. "I'll give you whatever you want."

"How about today I teach you the benefits of toys during a little mutual masturbation." She smiled up at him, and his heartbeat thundered in his ears. She had a deep dimple in her cheek, and he couldn't help but press his lips to it.

"Today? Will you teach me something different tomorrow?"

"If you're lucky."

"It could be the twelve days of Christmas sex toys. A new gizmo every day."

She chuckled, and he kissed her again. She tasted like his favorite wine.

When she pulled back for a breath, he sang, "*On the first day of Christmas, my …*"

They gazed at each other, stuck.

"My fuck buddy gave to me?" she suggested

Laughter bubbled up inside him, and her laughter followed until they were both giggling and holding each other up. She unbuttoned his jeans and shucked them to his knees. Suddenly sober, he yanked her toward him, and she wrapped one of her legs around his waist so his erection pressed against her core through their underwear.

"Watching you make yourself come would honestly be the hottest thing ever," he said, his voice ragged.

He'd never done that. Never watched someone or let someone watch him. The thought of having her eyes on him heightened the thrumming desire in his gut to almost unbearable levels.

His emotions were ping-ponging around, from giddiness to hair-on-fire lust. He couldn't keep up with himself.

A small smile tripped across her face. "Hold that thought."

She pulled out of his arms and rifled through her roller bag until she came up with a bottle of lube. Then she grabbed the dildo and Fleshstroker from the vanity.

"What's that one called?" he asked, nodding toward the slim, slightly curved dildo with a cute appendage popping off the side.

"The Double Trouble. I've never tried this one. You can help me christen it."

"Sure." His voice was faint, his mind reeling and skin prickling. She was going to burn him up before he'd even gotten his dick out. "What's it do? Besides the obvious."

"It's a vibrating dildo with a clitoral stimulator. The vibration is so strong it's supposed to feel like thrusting, so you'll have thrusting against your G-spot on the inside and pulsation against your clit on the outside at the same time. It's very popular. I created an awesome marketing campaign for it."

"I can imagine."

After a quick glance around the bathroom, she backed up against the far wall adjacent to the claw-foot tub. He shuffled after her, his pants around his knees.

Being disheveled and half undressed was weirdly doing it for him.

She pulled off her thong and handed it over. "Hold this."

"Oh. God. Okay." He wrapped the silky slip of fabric around his wrist and threaded his fingers into her short hair, tipping her head back. Red lipstick was slightly smeared around the corners of her lips from their kisses. "What next?"

"Pull your boxers down." Her voice was huskier than before.

He kept one hand in her hair and pushed his underwear down with the other, her thong tangled around his arm.

"Nice prick," she said. "Now watch."

Her eyelids fluttered and a breathy sigh slipped past her lush lips. She put the Double Trouble to use. The vibrator was nearly silent, but she certainly wasn't. She was sexy and vocal and completely debauched. Pink bloomed up her cheeks, and her mouth dropped open.

She propped one of her feet up on the lip of the bathtub. Her shiny pumps and sheer black stockings caught and held his attention as he let his free hand travel up her calf to her smooth, thick thigh.

"These leg things are doing something to me," he said. He traced the lacy top of the fishnet stockings. They had seams that ran down the back of her legs.

"They're called thigh-highs."

"I want to lick them. Want to lick all of you."

She moaned and pushed the toy in to the hilt. The

black silicone was vibrant against the pink of her pussy. Heat spread up his limbs, sparking in his gut. He grabbed his dick and sucked her bottom lip into his mouth.

This was too wild, but he'd never felt freer. Never felt so shocked by the touch of his own hand.

"Wait," she breathed. "Squirt some lube in here and use this." She held up the gold Fleshstroker. He hadn't realized she'd still been holding it.

The toy resembled a sparkly flashlight but with a slit on the end. He dribbled lube onto the opening, then balanced it on the tip of his dick. ·

"So, I just jerk off with this?" he asked.

Her breath was thundering out of her, the color high on her cheeks. She nodded. "Drive that cunt like you stole it, baby."

A shock of lust shot through him at her words, like lightning in his veins. Like hearing the word *cunt* drip from her dirty mouth had electrocuted him.

He pressed the Fleshstroker down over the head of his cock. A surprised grunt rumbled out of him.

She grinned. "Good, huh?"

"Holy shit." His knees shook as he stroked the toy down his length. The internal sleeve was silky and warm around him.

He fell against her hungrily, pushing her harder against the bathroom wall, and threaded his free hand back into her hair. Her foot was still propped up on the tub next to them, and he marveled over the way she'd opened up.

She moaned again, this time in her throat, as she took

his tongue into her mouth and sucked. A shudder worked its way up his spine and his balls tightened. He ripped his mouth away from her, totally dazed, and way too close. He slowed his hand and tried to breathe.

"So good, Sasha."

She flicked her gaze up, and it was full of humor and happiness and fun, but her mouth was slack with pleasure. Her hips twitched as she rode the toy harder, her movements precise and measured. She obviously knew exactly what she needed to make herself come. It was inspiring and sexy as hell.

"I love seeing my thong on your wrist," she said. "Hot watching you touch yourself."

He glanced down at her black panties wrapped around his arm. It pushed him closer to the edge, and he had to bite his lip to keep from shouting.

"Fuck, I can't believe how incredible this feels," he choked out.

"I'm really wet. And close." Her thigh trembled, and she tilted her head back against the wall, her neck bared to him. He mouthed at the hollow of her throat, then dragged his fingers from her hair, down the center of her chest, until they landed at the juncture of her body.

She wasn't simply wet around the toy. She drenched.

"Oh fuck." He traced his finger around the pulsing silicone bulb nestled against her clit. "Are you about to come?" he asked, his voice shot. She gasped and nodded, so he took a half-step back, his fingers still touching her slickness. "I want to be able to see you. Want to hear you."

He worked the Fleshstroker over himself harder. Faster. Their gazes snagged on each other, a moment of perfect eye contact, and a tiny piece of his heart snapped. This was better than he ever could have imagined, and he hated that it wasn't for keeps.

Suddenly, her breath hitched, her eyes closed, and her back bowed. She came apart on the Double Trouble, a tiny cry escaping, and it was so fucking gorgeous. So uninhibited.

The room spun. Warmth spread through his body, tension winding its way down his spine. He leaned in and kissed the sweet, sweaty join of her neck and shoulder and grabbed a handful of her ass. He was nearly there, right on the cusp of losing it.

"*Sasha?*" a voice called from the direction of the Blue Spruce Room. It was followed swiftly by a muffled knock.

"Shit. Fuck," Perry said under his breath. *His sister.* "Fuck."

Sasha removed her foot from the lip of the tub, crowding in his embrace, and slapped a hand over his mouth.

"This okay?" she asked him softly, breath hot in his ear. He nodded frantically. "Good. Go faster."

It was too much, too amazing. And the thrill of almost being caught, of having to be quiet—his eyes rolled back, his body shaking.

Right there. He was right there.

46

"Come for me, Perry," she whispered. Her teeth tugged his earlobe.

His body locked up, and she smothered his groan with her hand as he filled the Fleshstroker with his spunk.

It had only been a few seconds from the moment Valerie knocked, but he felt like time slowed as he quaked through his orgasm. His knees almost buckled, and his vision went as white as the blizzard outside.

"Hey, Valerie!" Sasha yelled to his sister in the other room, without lifting her hand from Perry's mouth. "Hold on. I'm in the bathroom." She casually held the Double Trouble in her other fist. It was wet and shiny from her arousal.

"Okay. I have the coziest, best pajamas in the world for you," Valerie said, her voice way too close for comfort. She was probably in the doorway to the Blue Spruce Room. They'd stupidly left it open.

Sasha dropped her hand from Perry's mouth. He caught her wrist and kissed her palm lightly. Something soft and maybe vulnerable flashed through her eyes before she backed away from him. He reached for her, but she neatly sidestepped him, wiggling until her dress fell back into place. After quickly fixing her hair where his hands had mussed it, she glanced at him in the mirror. She seemed totally unfazed. Calm and cool and not at all like she'd had an orgasm that had turned the room upside down.

Not like him. He couldn't see straight.

"Shit," he said again.

She started cleaning her vibrator off in the sink. He hadn't moved.

"Did I break you?" she whispered teasingly.

He shook his head. Then nodded.

"I'm guessing you don't want her to know, right?" Sasha said. "Your sister."

"No," he choked out. Of course he didn't want his sister to know he'd just jacked off.

With a bright gold Fancy Fleshstroker.

"Then you better lock this door behind me." She tilted her forehead toward his crotch. "You keep that, but I'd wash it out now rather than later." With that, she was out the door.

He stared down at the Fleshstroker and pulled it gingerly off his sensitive dick. It was messy with his come.

He was thankful Sasha wasn't there to see him blush.

Chapter Three

_S_asha slipped into her room and tried to calm
the pounding of her heart. She knew she was
flushed, but hopefully, Valerie wouldn't realize why.

"Hey!" Sasha said, too cheerfully. "Sorry about that."

Valerie was standing in the doorway of the room, half
in the hallway, clutching a pile of clothes.

"No problem. Sorry for taking so long rounding this
stuff up. I was finding pajamas for Louise, Andie, and
Karen too, which was a bit complicated since we're all
different sizes. Luckily, my ex left a bunch of sweats that
will fit Karen, little slip that she is."

Valerie chattered away, laying out the clothes she'd
found for Sasha. Sasha sat down next to her, which is
when she realized Perry must still have had her underwear wrapped around his wrist. She had to stifle a laugh.

What a bizarre day.

"Here are a couple pairs of sweats, some T-shirts, a
few sweatshirts, and several pairs of socks. I think it

should all fit you, since we're close to the same size, though the sweats might be too long. Also, here's a bag of travel-size toiletries."

Sasha peeked into the bag to see shampoo, soap, face wash, deodorant, toothpaste, and a toothbrush.

"I'm sure it'll work. I'm not picky."

"What's your shoe size?"

"Eight."

"Oh, that's good. I'll bring you slippers tomorrow so you have them if you need 'em. It sounds like we could be snowed in for a few days."

Sasha bit back a groan, not wanting to insult Valerie and her hospitality. There were worse places to be stranded than a nice B and B, but *damn*. This place was so Christmassy it rolled her stomach. At least she'd found a fuck buddy.

One who made her feel open and soft, which was an indication that sleeping with Perry was a huge mistake.

She didn't do vulnerable.

"I'm sorry I'm stranded. I hope you're not going to too much trouble for me."

"Nah. It'll be fun. Some of my fondest memories as a kid are getting snowed in here with quirky guests and my mom and grandparents and Perry. As teenagers, we got stuck here on New Year's Eve once. You'd have thought the world was ending, I was so devastated. I didn't get to kiss my secret girlfriend at midnight. Perry made me spiked hot chocolate and watched chick flicks with me." She laughed. "God, he was such a sweet kid."

Imagining Perry and Valerie as teenagers running

around this place—it couldn't have been further from her childhood. Raised by an overworked and underpaid grandma. Parents out of the picture. A home full of hardships.

But love too. Her grandma had filled Sasha's life with so much love, and she missed her every day, especially this time of year.

"Perry seems like a sweet adult as well. He gave me wine and chocolate cake." And the best kisses she'd had in ages. And a pretty rocking orgasm.

"Yeah. He's the romantic in the family," Valerie said with a mischievous smile.

Uh-oh. That was not what Sasha wanted to hear.

A slightly awkward silence followed at that. Sasha cleared her throat and stared at the floor.

"Well, I'll let you get to sleep." Valerie snapped back into her role as host. "My chef won't be able to come in with the weather so bad, so breakfast is all on me tomorrow. I'll serve at nine, but if you're early or late, no problem. We'll get you fixed up, I promise. Any food allergies or sensitivities?"

Sasha shook her head.

"Okay. Goodnight, Sasha. If you need anything, my number is on the pad of paper on your bedside table. And Perry is next door. He can help you too."

"Thank you. I really appreciate everything you're doing for me."

"Of course." Valerie gave her another one of those quick hugs, and like the first time, it choked Sasha up with emotion.

Once she was alone, she changed into a pair of velour sweats and a T-shirt, then fell back onto her bed. There was a small water spot on the ceiling, and it filled her with relief. She wasn't sure she could handle this cozy-ass place if there weren't some underlying imperfections to cut the flawlessness.

Christmas lights wrapped around the posts of the bed and flickered through the filmy canopy curtains. She was too exhausted and satisfied to get up and turn the twinkle lights off.

She should go retrieve her Double Trouble from the bathroom counter, but she didn't want to run into Perry. Plus, if she left it there, it would give him something to think about. She liked that idea a lot.

Thinking about Perry made her simultaneously nervous and excited. Mid-orgasm Perry was her new favorite Perry. He'd been delightfully tousled, his hair a mess of sweat-damp curls and his clothes all askew.

She suddenly wished that they'd done something that was a little more naked, more horizontal. She wanted to see his whole, long body on display.

Wanted that exposed feeling of being naked together, of skin on bare skin.

Talk about a red flag.

At least Valerie had presented an easy escape, a way to disengage. If Valerie hadn't knocked, Sasha would probably have taken an extra second to stare, then an extra second to kiss him.

Perry's enticing sweetness was a disaster waiting to

happen, so thank God they were on the same, no-strings page.

With that last thought in her head, she snuggled down into the softest, most comfortable bed ever. Then she fell asleep.

SASHA WOKE UP TO A BLARING, God-awful noise coming from her cell phone.

She groggily stared at her screen. It was a weather alert.

An extended Blizzard Warning.

She tossed the phone toward her bedside table, but there was no bedside table there. Her phone hit a wall. She sat up straight in bed.

Where the fuck was she?

"Oh, no."

Falling back onto the bed, she buried her head under a pillow. The Winterberry Inn.

That was why her room smelled like cinnamon and spruce trees. As the sound of the shower in the connected en suite shut off, warmth hit her cheeks and spread heat down her body. Perry must be in there.

Naked.

Seeing a naked Perry wouldn't be a bad way to start the morning. But the bed was so comfortable, so snug.

Instead of propositioning Perry again, she grabbed

her phone from the floor, slid deeper under the plaid flannel covers, and texted her brother, Benji.

Sasha: *I need advice.*

Benji: *Oh, girl talk?*

Sasha rolled her eyes. Benji texted her again before she could respond.

Benji: *I recommend the Rimmy. Whoever your partner is will love it.*

She laughed. The Rimmy was a Lady Robin's butt plug. It had beads that moved around the neck, which was supposed to mimic the feel of being rimmed. Her brother was a menace.

Sasha: *I'm stuck in a Hallmark movie. There's a Christmas tree in my room, and I bet I get bullied into singing carols by the end of the day. What the hell should I do?*

She fully expected Benji, her cynical little brother, to tell her to slick on black nail polish and embrace her hatred of the season. Her siblings knew how much Christmas got to her. They'd been there during the fallout of her broken engagement, had helped pick her up when she was sure she'd never get out of bed, and had trashed thousands of dollars of Christmas wedding decorations for her so she'd never have to see them again.

Benji: *Fa la la la la, bitch.*

Well, he was a dead end.

Sasha: *I should have asked the divorcée.*

Benji: *Only if you wanted to listen to Rosie fuss over you.*

Sasha groaned. A meddling, worried sister was the last thing she needed.

Sasha: *You suck.*

Benji: *Like a pro.*

She wrinkled her nose.

Sasha: *That's enough of that. Are you at your apartment? Do you have all the bread and milk you'll need?*

As Sasha checked up on her brother—he had two older sisters who loved to fuss over him—ensuring he wasn't going to starve during the snow-pocalypse, thin light started to filter through her window. She crawled out of bed and peeked outside. It was a solid white hellscape.

Another day in holiday paradise.

Once the shower shut off and she heard Perry's door to the bathroom close, she snuck into the en suite. Her Double Trouble was still on the counter, which filled her with ridiculous giddiness.

She grabbed the toy and brought it into the shower with her. It was waterproof after all. As the water rushed over her head, she let her mind wander and rubbed the vibrator over her clit. Images flashed through her mind, some fragmented and disjointed. She conjured up the lips, the eyes, the smile of a woman she'd slept with last month.

She pushed the Double Trouble inside her pussy, upping the vibration.

Good, so good.

A different smile hit her unexpectedly. Perry's.

The huskiness of his voice. The uninhibited ring of his laugh. His open, expressive face.

Oh fuck.

Heat ripped through her as more images of him burst through her brain.

The corded muscles in his neck standing in stark relief. The bones of his hand as it worked the Fancy Fleshstroker. His eyes rolling back. His fingertips slipping through the slickness of her arousal.

She had to bite her wrist to muffle her cries as she came.

Once the ripples of pleasure began to ebb, she slumped against the wall of the shower in shock. She was officially giving the Double Trouble her stamp of approval.

But where Perry Winters was concerned, she was so fucked.

She finished showering, using shampoo and soap that smelled like peppermint, because of course even the toiletries in this place were Christmas-themed. Out of the clothes Valerie had lent her, she chose a pair of loose sweatpants and a sweatshirt that said *Matriarchy Knows Best.*

When she finally made it downstairs, Valerie and Perry were in the kitchen cooking cherry-stuffed French toast together. From the doorway of the kitchen, Sasha watched as Valerie hip-bumped Perry out of the way. They laughed and teased each other, until Valerie started singing a Christmas carol.

Hell no. Sasha was *out.* She wasn't sure she could deal with either Valerie's Christmas cheer or Perry's morning sexiness.

She turned and ran smack-dab into Louise, who was fresh faced and had snow in her hair.

"Oh!" Sasha said. "I'm sorry. I didn't see you."

"It's okay. I just braved the trek from the carriage house. I've never seen snow this bad. It's up to my knees out there. I'm all wind-whipped."

"I'm guessing it's too bad to drive, then," Sasha said glumly. She'd been hoping she could make it home today, but their snowed-in status was only worsening.

"Definitely, even if our cars could make it up the driveway. The newscasters this morning were saying the interstate is shut down between here and the city because they can't get crews out there to rescue people who get stranded."

"Good morning, ladies," Valerie called from the kitchen, evidently spotting them. "Oh, Louise, you're a snow angel!"

Louise blushed prettily and glanced down with a grin.

That was interesting.

"Good morning," Sasha said. "How'd you guys sleep?"

Perry shot her a tiny, ironic smile. "Like a baby."

"Great." Sasha glanced at Valerie. "And you?"

"Awesome. That early Christmas present I bought myself was a great investment."

Sasha snorted, easily catching Valerie's meaning. Perry wasn't so quick.

"What'd you buy yourself?" He was concentrating on stirring some kind of cream and cherry mixture.

"A vibrator."

Perry's head snapped up and he dropped his spoon into the bowl. His gaze traveled between Sasha and

Valerie. "Oh." A deep blush spread over his cheeks and down his neck. "I did not need to know that."

"Nope, but you asked, ding dong," Valerie said.

Sasha, Louise, and Valerie all laughed at his obvious discomfort. Sasha felt almost honored that everyone had had such a nice sex-toy-filled evening.

"Perry, why don't you get Sasha and Louise coffee or tea?" Valerie said.

He nodded, seemingly grateful to escape the teasing. He got Sasha and Louise set up in the breakfast room with the fanciest, tastiest coffee Sasha had ever had. Within thirty minutes, the room was full of the other guests.

It was mostly couples. Only one family had kids, and they had a brood of four. They ranged in age from a toddler to a teenager who reminded Sasha of Benji at that age. Black clothing, dyed black hair, eyeliner. She wanted to ask the kid if he liked My Chemical Romance.

At least there was one other person who seemed as disgusted by the Christmas cheer as she was.

Valerie floated into the breakfast room on a wave of sweet-smelling baked goods. "Okay folks, we have cherry-stuffed French toast, applewood-smoked bacon and facon, for the vegetarians in the group, buttermilk biscuits, apricot preserves, and eggs made to order." Valerie and Perry laid out platters of food on the tables family-style.

It all looked too good to eat, but she'd manage. Some-how. Sasha loaded up a plate with French toast, bacon, and a hard-fried egg. As everyone else was serving them-selves, Perry sat down next to her.

Sasha tried to focus on the food in front of her, so she wouldn't ogle the man beside her. The French toast was buttery, the cherry stuffing tart enough to cut the sweetness of the syrup. It was probably the best meal she'd had in ages, which wasn't a surprise considering she more or less lived on popcorn, chips and salsa, and grilled cheese sandwiches. And Indian takeout. Lots and lots of takeout.

On her second bite, she failed at stifling a moan, which made Perry jerk beside her.

Oops.

She licked her fork and shot him a wink. He practically growled and squeezed her knee under the table. Heat spread up her leg and settled in her stomach.

He leaned in and whispered, "You're being naughty."

She smiled, oddly pleased, then glanced up to catch Karen and Andie watching them, assessing them. Sasha didn't like that at all. The newlyweds were plotting.

"Alrighty, guests!" Valerie said from the front of the room. Both Perry and Sasha jerked, and Perry yanked his hand away. "As you can see, a few people weren't able to make it home due to the weather after last night's private party, and we're stranded until at least tomorrow. The interstate is closed down from here all the way into the city, so we're stuck. Luckily, I've been planning Christmassy snowed-in activities in my head for years!"

The teenager groaned so Sasha didn't have to. *Ah, a kindred spirit.*

Valerie didn't slow down for one second. "I have a bunch of made-for-TV Christmas movies cued up in the den. I'll be baking gingersnaps and sugar cookies later today, and anyone can join me. We'll also have an orna-ment-making station here in the breakfast room after lunch. Lastly, if you want to brave the blizzard to sled in the backyard, the hill down to the carriage house is fantastic. Of course, you're welcome to get up to your own brand of fun. There are board games, books, maga-zines, and DVDs in the den that are yours for the taking. You have free reign of the entire house, except for other people's rooms, so make yourself at home."

Everyone broke apart after that. Perry stood and stretched, giving Sasha an eye-level view of his treasure trail, which she managed not to lick. Barely.

Maybe they could fuck all day.

No one was watching so she lightly traced his hipbone with a fingertip. He jumped a mile, then grinned at her.

"I think I'm going to head back to my room," she said, giving him a pointed look. "Maybe braid my hair or take a nap." Never mind that her hair was way too short for braids and she'd just woken up from an awesome night's sleep.

He nodded. "Yeah, braids. I'm good with that."

"Great."

She stood from her seat at the table, ready to escape for some playtime. Maybe she'd show Perry the Rimmy after all. She was pretty sure she had one that hadn't sold the night before. She could expense it.

Valerie appeared beside her and looped her arms through Sasha's and Perry's elbows.

"Perry, guess which movie I have ready to go first this morning. It's your favorite."

"*My Amnesiac Christmas?*"

"Yep!"

Sasha stared at Perry in horror and admiration. He was kind of a weirdo, and she kind of liked that.

He smiled shyly. "What? I love tropes."

Valerie laughed and pushed them toward the den. "You better get in there to watch it before Karen puts on ESPN. I promised Louise Christmas movies, but she'll be too shy to speak up if someone changes the channel."

Perry shot Valerie a mock glare. "You need to promise Louise something else. Like a date."

So it *was* like that. Sasha had wondered.

"*Shhh.* I'm working on it," Valerie said, matching his semi-seriousness. "These things take finesse. She's skittish. Now get out of here. I need to clean up."

"I could help you," Sasha said. She'd rather do the dishes than watch Christmas movies. And she hated dishes. In fact, maybe being snowed-in here in the Christmas-verse was worth it to escape the mountain of dishes at her own place.

"Nah, you go on. I prefer to clean on my own. Gives me time to think." Valerie playfully pushed them from the room.

"I hope this isn't a trend," Sasha said glumly as they trudged into the den.

"What?" Perry asked.

"Getting cock blocked."

Unfortunately, it was a trend.

Every time Sasha and Perry tried to sneak away in the coming hours, they were pulled into a different Winter

Wonderland activity. Sasha gritted her teeth through two Christmas movies—*My Amnesiac Christmas* and *Toyland's Secret Baby*. They got talked into icing sugar cookies next, then Karen and Andie dragged them into the sitting room with the piano to sing carols with Valerie and Louise.

After an off-key, and off-color, rendition of "Santa Baby," Sasha tried to edge toward the exit. She was not a singer, and she certainly wasn't enjoying this.

As if sensing her escape, Andie turned around from the keyboard and said to Sasha, "You trade places with Karen."

Karen, who had a rocking singing voice, grinned and shuffled Sasha into her spot.

Now she was farther from the door and freedom.

Next they sang "Silver Bells." Sasha's teeth hurt it was so sweet. Everyone seemed so happy, and she was miserable.

"Sasha, why don't you take another step back. You're blocking my light a little," Andie said, which was frankly untrue, but Sasha would do anything to get away from the singing. "Perry, you're a baritone, aren't you? You should go stand by Sasha."

What did him being a baritone have to do with her?

Perry flicked his gaze up at the ceiling and Sasha followed his eyes.

Mistletoe.

Andie had been maneuvering her underneath the mistletoe.

Sasha scowled. She was perfectly happy fucking

around with Perry, but she was not falling prey to any holiday matchmaking.

Relationships weren't her thing. She wanted nothing to do with the sugar plum hearts dancing in Andie's eyes. The women in the room were watching the drama play out with glee.

"Stop it," Sasha said, and everyone laughed. "I think I'm done singing. If you'll excuse me."

She escaped the nightmare caroling. Perry caught up with her before she reached the Blue Spruce Room.

"I'm sorry about that," he said, touching her shoulder lightly. "I didn't have anything to do with it." He sighed. "Well, maybe they can see that I'm kind of lost over how much I like you, but I didn't put them up to it."

She stared up at him. "You shouldn't like me. I'm not girlfriend material."

"I didn't ask you to be my girlfriend. I know where you stand, Sasha."

"Once the snow-pocalypse is over so is this." She gestured between them.

The muscle in his jaw twitched almost imperceptibly. "*I know*. Doesn't mean I don't like you. I think I'm allowed." He smiled at her, and she was lost herself. All it took was a flash of his straight, white teeth to make her soften.

Damn it.

He cupped her cheek gently. "Come on. I want to show you my favorite room in the house. It's a secret room."

"Really?"

"Yeah, and you're going to love it."

"Why?" she asked.

"It's the only room Val doesn't decorate for Christmas."

She closed her eyes. Oh man, someone was getting his dick sucked later.

"Lead the way."

Chapter Four

---

*S*asha slipped into the Blue Spruce Room to discreetly grab a handful of … uh … implements before following Perry up to the third floor. Luckily, the baggy sweats and sweatshirt she was wearing had large pockets.

Once they reached the third floor, Perry stopped in front of the door at the end of the hallway. It was locked, but he had a key. He opened the door, which led to narrow, steep stairs.

"We're not going to find your wife locked away up there, are we?"

He glanced over his shoulder with a confused smile. "Huh? No. I'm not married."

"Nor Mr. Rochester's wife?"

Perry's laugh echoed through the stairway. "No, but I'm sure there is a copy of *Jane Eyre*."

"*Ooo*, exciting!"

The room came slowly into view, and it took her breath away.

It was a huge attic room with a pitched cedar roof and white shiplap walls. Someone had built bookshelves into the large triangle-shaped wall at the end of the room, and there was an old-fashioned record player next to retro blue velvet furniture. The floor was a dark wood, but their footsteps were muffled by a soft white rug.

A door off to the right caught Sasha's eye. She pushed it open to find a small shower and bathroom. God, this was all the space she'd ever need. It was perfect.

"I love it."

Perry's warm smile was worth the price of admission for this whole stupid snowed-in adventure.

"This is where my grandparents lived until it was too hard for them to make it up the stairs. Once Valerie took over the daily operations of the inn, she turned it into a personal library."

"What about your parents? Where are they?"

"My dad passed when we were young. My mom and Valerie eventually took over until Valerie was experienced enough to run it on her own. I own quite a large share of it, but it's Valerie's baby. We grew up in the carriage house with Grandma and Grandpa up here. Now our mom is living it up in Hawaii with her much younger boyfriend." Perry laughed, like he couldn't be happier for his mother, and sat down on the blue sofa.

Sasha moved toward the bookshelves. The books were arranged by genre, and unsurprisingly, a large portion were romances. She trailed a finger over a row of cracked spines.

"And you live in Topeka and do what, exactly? I want to hear about your complicated living situation," she said. These were probably topics they should have covered before their little bathroom foray last night, but she'd been able to tell Perry's job was a sensitive subject for him, so she'd let the opportunity to learn more pass her by. To be honest, she normally knew someone better before she fooled around with them. Most of her partners in the last year, as well as the years before her failed engagement, had been friends, with only a handful of one-night stands mixed in.

The corners of his mouth tipped down, and a wrinkle formed between his eyebrows.

"I was a CPA, but I got laid off at the beginning of December." He stared up at the ceiling, seeming to select his words carefully. "I didn't see it coming. They cut the accounting department by a third and eliminated all the middle managers like me. They'd lost a big client and decided it'd be cheaper to outsource the work."

"That's a horrible thing to happen right before Christmas."

He nodded, his lips tight. "I was overcome by this horrendous *relief* afterward."

"Oh."

"Yeah." He smiled sadly. "I didn't like my job, and I don't think that's an issue that'll be fixed by getting a new job as an accountant for some other company. So when I was pulled into that office and my life was turned upside down, I thought there must be something wrong with me because I was elated. I could breathe again. I felt as if a door had been opened."

"Maybe it has."

"I haven't told Valerie yet. She'll worry over me, and I wasn't ready for that. I needed to make a plan first, you know? Of course, my plan involves moving in with her. I should have asked her before I sold my furniture, packed the rest of my life into my SUV, and showed up in a snowstorm, huh?"

Sasha laughed. "I've always heard Christmas is a great time to make huge, life-changing decisions."

He chuckled and scrubbed his hands down his face. "My girlfriend broke up with me after I lost my job. She didn't understand why I'd put everything on the line, waste all my severance package, to chase a misshapen dream. It made me feel like I couldn't trust my instincts about people. I'd thought we were solid together."

Her thoughts rebelled at the relationship talk, so she steered the conversation away from it. "What's your dream?"

She sat down next to him. He reached up and thumbed her bottom lip. The tug of his skin against hers resonated deep inside, like he'd plucked the harp string of her heart.

"Flowers."

"Flowers?"

"And trees. Horticulture, basically. I enrolled in a horticulture and landscape architecture program at the college in the city. I want to own my own landscaping company one day."

"Wow. That wasn't what I expected."

He smiled, his thumb still on her mouth. "You wouldn't be surprised if you'd seen me naked."

That shocked a laugh out of her. "Oh, is that so, mister? Are you made of tree bark?"

"No. Ink."

He stood suddenly, right as her greedy hands were reaching to rip his clothes off. Nothing got her hotter than tattoos.

She watched him as he fiddled with the record player. His back flexed as he lifted a record onto the stand. His shoulders were wide and strong, his waist narrow, his butt mouth-watering.

When he turned back toward her, she snapped her gaze up from his derrière.

He grinned. "Dance with me."

"What? No." That skirted way too close to romance for her.

Slow, sultry music filled the room. Eartha Kitt. At least it wasn't her Christmas stuff.

"Come on. It's foreplay." He pulled her up off the couch and into his arms. For one terrifying second, everything in the world felt *right*. Felt *good*. She melted against him. Maybe she could give in a little. Just until the end of the song.

Sasha pressed their bodies together, slid her hands under the hem of his flannel shirt until she could touch his hot skin, and brushed her mouth against his bearded jaw. His hands threaded into her hair.

The song was in French, and she had no idea what the words meant, but it was full of tenderness and yearning. She kissed him, trying to stem the rising tide of longing rushing in her blood. They swayed to the beat.

"What's in the pocket of your sweatshirt?" he murmured against her lips. "Feels like a dick."

"It is."

He kissed her harder, the slick, suggestive thrust of his tongue into her mouth weakening her knees. His hand snuck into the kangaroo pocket of her hoodie, then tossed the dildo onto the couch.

"What's in your sweatpants pockets?"

"Wouldn't you like to know," she said tartly, as she unbuttoned the top buttons of his flannel shirt, then lifted it over his head.

His skin glowed golden in the dim light of the attic, and she sluiced her hands over the muscles of his shoulders and back. He lifted one large palm up to grip her jaw and hold her steady as he kissed her. She caught a one-second glimpse of a tatted arm sleeve in muted, earthy colors. His other hand crept under her sweatshirt and trembled down the line of her spine.

They rocked through one whole song, then another, their mouths fused together. Sasha was dizzy with want by the time Perry slid her sweatshirt over her head. As she pulled back to catch a breath, his arms still tangled around her, she got a better glimpse of his tattoos. His arm sleeve was all wildflowers, and he had a large magenta peony on his ribs.

She pressed a hand to the peony, and he gasped.

He was beautiful. His chest and stomach were rough with dark hair, his lips wet from their kisses, his cheeks flushed.

They kissed and touched for the space of another song, their skin pressed together, until Sasha couldn't handle it anymore.

She pulled away. "I need … God, Perry."

Perry slipped a hand into her sweatpants pocket and found the nipple clamps, which Sasha had branded the Chained Melody Clamps due to the alternating black and white metal chain length that mirrored piano keys. His eyes got wide and wild, his face even more flushed.

She shucked his pajama bottoms and boxers off, and he stepped out of them. He had tattooed vines twisting up his calves and painting his thighs.

His body was a garden and one of the nicest she'd ever seen.

"Sit down," she said roughly. He sat on the sofa as if someone had cut his legs out from underneath him. "And buckle up."

He grinned, almost helplessly, like he couldn't control his reactions to her.

That grin echoed through her mind minutes later as she was kneeling between Perry's legs and sucking on the blunt tip of his dick, edging him to oblivion.

She took him a bit deeper and cupped his heavy,

meaty balls. He spread his legs wider and let go of a desperate whine. She popped off his dick.

Time to up the ante.

Without warning, she leaned forward and sucked on one of his nipples. She'd noticed that needy glint in his eye when he'd found the clamps, and she suspected he was desperate for them.

He cried out when her lips touched the sensitive nub, first one and then the other. She suckled and bit them until they were dusky rose and hard. Then she lifted the clamps off the couch. The Chained Melody Clamps were tweezer-style with silicone pinchers and a weighted connector chain. Great for beginners, not too rough, and easy to pull off.

She rubbed a fingertip around his nipple. "Do you want this?"

"*Yes.*"

She watched his face closely as she clipped the first one on. His breath hissed out of him like a teakettle.

"Still good?"

"Uh-huh. Very."

She snapped the other one on, and his back bowed, his hips rising off the couch.

"What do you want, Perry?" she asked as she kissed his chin.

"Your mouth. On me, on my ..." He shivered against her.

"On your what?" Humor laced her voice, especially as he groaned brokenly, unable to answer.

She kissed down his chest and rubbed her cheek in his

hair. The mix of a thick pelt on his chest and beautiful botanicals on his skin made her lose her head. She loved hairy masc people. Every once in a while, she craved smooth skin, and curves, and softness. But sometimes she was in the mood to press her face into some unruly body hair, and holy hell, did Perry have that in spades.

She returned to his cock and licked a stripe up the vein before tonguing his slit. He placed his hands in her hair but didn't fist it or pull her onto his cock. She liked a lover with restraint. She glanced up and made eye contact.

His breathing was erratic, his eyes wide and unwavering from her face. She'd been torturing him for so long now that his body was strung tight and damp with sweat. He'd not once complained or given any indication that he wasn't thoroughly enjoying it, though.

The vine of his tattoo snaked around the top of his thigh to his hipbone, and she followed it with her fingernail. He groaned when she reached the smooth skin over bone.

"Didn't know … that was an erogenous zone until you." He trailed his hand down the back of her neck, and she sucked his crown, sighing at the burst of salt on her tongue. "Close. Getting close, Sasha."

She pulled off with an obscene pop, and he finally, *finally*, moaned out his frustration.

"How's it feel?" she asked. "The clamps."

"Sexy. Feels like I'm close to you, using toys with you. Ones you picked."

She froze, shocked by his honesty and the vulnerability rushing through her at his words. That hadn't been her intention with this, but maybe she should've anticipated bonus emotions with Perry. She'd expected this to be a sexy little game but now was sure she'd misjudged.

She looked him in the eye as she wrapped the weighted chain connecting the clamps around her index finger. He groaned when she tugged on the chain lightly.

"I'm going to yank these off when you come. Are you ready for that?"

He nodded very seriously. "Yes, beautiful."

Oh, he was such a gem.

She laughed and sucked him back down, getting sloppy with it. He cried out and tensed.

"Right there. I'm right there," he chanted.

As that first splash of jizz hit her tongue, she ruthlessly jerked the chain until she heard the snap as the clamps popped off his nipples.

The noise he made was unreal as he flooded her mouth. Harsh and shocked and broken. After several shivering seconds, his hips twisted and he cupped her cheeks, gently pulling her off.

"Was that okay?" she asked after swallowing, holding the nipple clamps up.

"Yes." He was out of breath but managed halting sentences. "It hurt so badly ... and felt so incredible ... like my pleasure and pain receptors were going haywire. I loved it."

They gazed at each other for a long moment. Then Perry snuck his hands under her arms and lifted her into his lap. He was all sweaty and flushed.

"You're beautiful," he said again, but this time she had trouble laughing it off. She felt oddly defenseless with his taste on her lips.

"Sweet-talker."

"You bet. Now it's your turn." He kissed her fiercely for long reality-shaking minutes but caught her hand as she tried to dip it to her pussy. Need was throbbing through her, harsh and alarming.

He tumbled her down onto her back with her head on the arm of the sofa, then pulled her sweatpants off.

"Commando today?" he murmured, gobbling up her body with his gaze.

She'd landed on the dildo, so she tugged it out from underneath her and tossed it to him. "The only pair of panties I had ended up on your wrist last night. Do your worst." Maybe if he made her come, if he focused all his formidable energy on her pleasure, she'd be able to recover some of those emotional walls she depended on, because they were dropping fast.

Maybe if she made this all about sex, he wouldn't see how his sweetness cracked through her, found her soft center, and ripped her apart.

Perry sat up on his knees between her legs. "So wet for me already." His voice was deep and rough, as if his control had shattered.

He stared down at her until she squirmed. "I love giving head," he said. "Want to feel you come on my face."

"*Fuck*," she whispered.

"What do you want?"

"That, Perry. I want *that*!"

"I plan to take my time. Make you my afternoon snack."

"Who are you?" she asked with a laugh, and he smiled.

He kissed down her midline, over her pubic bone, and before his mouth connected with her clit, he hummed happily. Then he buried his face between her legs.

She'd expected him to be shyer. To fiddle around and get his bearings.

He didn't need to get his bearings, it seemed. His mouth found her like a target. He sucked on her clit, trying different pressures, testing her to see what made her breathless, what made her writhe. In a matter of minutes, her head was spinning. The ache in her clit was sharp-edged and perfect. His tongue was heavenly. He pulled back, causing her to whine.

"You taste so fucking good." His free hand skimmed up her calf.

She groaned and buried her fingers in his dark curls. "Keep going."

He fell back onto her, his mouth focused. The caress of his thumb between the wet, swollen lips of her pussy surprised her. He teased her, his thumb right at her opening but not pressing inside, lighting up all those oft-ignored nerve endings.

He kept up the soft stroke of his thumb and licked her clit. Blood rushed from her head, and her vision went fuzzy.

Then the dildo was there. It was a short but fat metal

dildo called the Rude Beast. One of her favorites from Lady Robin's when she wanted something weighty. He drove it inside her, helped along by her slickness, and she gasped at the sudden fullness.

He licked around the toy, grinding it against her G-spot gently, before returning his focus to her clit.

"Like that," she breathed. "Exactly like that." And thank the Ghost of Orgasms Present, because he didn't take that command as an instruction to go harder or faster, which was her biggest sex pet peeve ever. Bliss buzzed down her spine. Her clit and pussy throbbed. "Close. *Oh God.* Perry. Don't stop."

The last stroke of tongue, the one that did her in, was accompanied by an impossibly sweet growl from Perry. Smarting, aching pleasure contracted into a pinprick on the verge of explosion. She screamed hoarsely, once, releasing all that abandon and desire into the dimly lit attic as her orgasm shook her.

When she could see again, when she could hear more than the echoes of her cry, she realized she was fisting his hair so tightly it had to hurt, but he appeared unconcerned. He lapped at her as he pulled the Rude Beast out. His tongue dipped to her cunt and delved inside, like he couldn't help but taste her pleasure, couldn't help but feel the last ripples of her climax on his tongue.

Before it became too much, he lifted his head away and sat up. His eyes were molten and dark, and she couldn't look away. She felt taken over by him, consumed by his intense gaze, as he lifted the Rude Beast to her mouth and painted her bottom lip with her arousal. Her tongue snaked out on its own, licking it up.

Then he popped the dildo into his own mouth, sucking the rest of her juices off it. His beard was wet from her, his lips swollen.

She stared at him, totally floored. He smiled.

Chapter Five

---

*P*erry watched Sasha come down from her orgasm and plotted.

He wanted a date, and it should have been the simplest thing to ask for. She might say no.

Okay, she'd *already* said no.

He'd read enough romances to know that a good grovel could go a long way, but he didn't really have anything to grovel for. Maybe a better plan would be to beg. Or execute a grand gesture.

He suspected none of those things would work on her. The romance novels he'd read had left him completely unprepared for this.

He evidently wasn't made for no-strings arrangements. All she'd had to do was hand him a sex toy, and he was ready to start talking about the future. It might as well have been a ring.

She'd made sex fun, and he hadn't had that in a long time. Sex had always been serious business. He wanted the laughing, the adventure, the eye-opening intimacy. *And* he wanted the girl.

With one last suck on the short, heavy dildo, he let it slip from his lips and tossed it behind him. The heft of it in his mouth had been obscene and dirty. And weirdly perfect. He didn't think he had any desire to suck an actual penis but putting a fake one in his mouth had made him hot all over. Judging by Sasha's dark, shocked expression, she'd been equally affected.

A slow grin spread across her face, and he was help-less to do anything but stare until the desire in him turned into a different type of longing. He couldn't keep it inside.

"Sasha, I like you. What can I do to make you—"

She touched a finger to his mouth, silencing him. "Don't ruin it."

"Okay." His voice wavered, and he put some space between them. He needed to not be naked right now.

"Perry, I'm sorry."

He waved her off with a fake smile. "It's okay." He tossed her clothes to her, and they both got dressed. "I'm sorry I made it weird."

She tipped her head back and peered at the pitched ceiling. "I can't feel my toes yet."

He laughed, pleased she was still reeling, and sat down beside her. She had a distinct way of putting people at ease without revealing anything about herself, and he wanted to know everything. Why she didn't date, why she hated Christmas, why her eyes seemed to scream each time he was tender or sweet toward her, how she got into the sex-toy industry. Everything.

But those topics were ones you eased into, ones you told friends or lovers, not strangers who you were fucking to pass the time during a snow-pocalypse.

Sasha's gaze drifted to the bookshelf spilling over with paperbacks. "I have a theory about what your favorite romance subgenre might be," she said.

"Oh yeah?"

"Historical romance." She turned back toward him in time to see him wrinkle his nose. She chuckled. "I'm that wrong?"

"A bit."

"You sometimes talk like an old-timey hero." He barked out a surprised laugh, and she ran a fingertip along his bearded jaw. "And you kind of look like a Mr. Darcy. All mysterious and dark haired, as if you should be walking along the rainy moors. Except you're too smiley."

"I'm sorry to disappoint, but you're wrong."

"What's your favorite?"

"I think you'll be surprised."

"Hit me. I'll brace myself."

"Paranormal. Shifters, to be specific."

A huge grin stretched her cheeks. She was so fucking gorgeous.

"I love that," she said. "What's the best book you've read recently?"

"I read a novella last week where the heroine was a bear shifter. She was big, bossy, and queer. There was a bit of a love triangle, which a lot of readers hate but I love. It was funny. I enjoy funny books."

"Gosh, that gives me so much insight into you. Valerie said you're the romantic in the family."

He glanced away from her, trying not to give himself away or make things awkward again. He had all these romantic ideals but had always been horrible at the follow-through, as evidenced by his line of breakups.

Maybe he'd just never been with the right person, the type of person who made him comfortable in his own skin, comfortable with sex and intimacy, comfortable letting loose the romantic in his heart.

Crazy that he was sure Sasha could be that woman, if she'd allow it.

He knew that she wouldn't. She'd made that clear.

"Your turn. I'm the romantic in the family and love bear shifters. Tell me something I don't know about you."

Sasha considered his question for a long time before shrugging. "You might not want to keep hanging out after I tell you this"

He couldn't imagine what she'd say that might make him feel that way.

"You've already admitted to drinking boxed wine. What could be worse?"

She laughed and jokingly punching his arm. "Nothing, evidently. I'm bisexual."

Now it was his turn to laugh. "I'd figured that out."

"Really?"

"Yeah, Valerie told me she thought you were queer. She has good gaydar." He paused thoughtfully. "What do you call that if you're bi? Bi-dar?"

"Queer-dar?" she provided helpfully.

"Is that what you say?"

"No, I say gaydar."

He bumped his shoulder against hers. She continued to blow him away with her wit, and humor, and courage. Every moment he spent in her presence made him like her more, want her more.

He was in awe of his sister and her bravery in coming out and living authentically. Valerie hadn't had the easiest time as a teenager, but she was the strongest person he knew. It took guts to come out, and it was a constant process, reoccurring every time you met someone new. He doubted he'd have the strength or patience to do that.

"Thank you for telling me," he said.

"Some people I've been with have had issues with it."

Those assholes. He brushed a lock of hair off her forehead.

"That's horrible. I'm sorry. I don't have a problem with it in the least, if that means anything to you."

She smiled and pressed her head into his fingertips. "It means more than you can imagine."

"Is that why you don't date?" he asked.

"No. That's a whole other thing. So how did you get interested in landscaping and horticulture?"

He blinked a few times, trying to adjust to the abrupt subject change. "I could show you."

"I'd love that."

"We'll have to leave the only Christmas-free zone in the house."

"Oh, never mind, then." They shared a comfortable laugh before Sasha hauled herself off the couch. "Kidding. Lead the way. We've probably missed lunch, and I'm starving."

She moved around languidly, like she was satisfied, and a burst of pride hit him. He loved seeing her like that and knowing he'd caused it with nothing but his mouth and a toy.

They made their way out of the attic, with a quick pit stop in the Blue Spruce Room to stash the toys, then to the ground floor of the inn. The place was alive with activities and warmth. The stranded members of the Staunchly Raunchy Book Club were playing gin rummy in front of the fire in the hearth room and several other guests were watching football.

He and Sasha avoided everyone as they traversed the house. He didn't want to answer any questions about where they'd disappeared to.

He pulled her into the formal dining room, which had huge windows that overlooked the backyard. From those windows, the carriage house and the rest of the property was visible. The family with the kids was in the backyard building a snowman as flurries whipped around them. He'd never seen snow that thick.

"Okay, you ready for this?" he asked her as he directed her in front of one of the windows.

She nodded. "Born ready."

He pointed at the gazebo. "That gazebo is surrounded by hydrangea bushes I planted the summer after I graduated high school. I love the way they pop against the white of the gazebo, but they can be finicky. In the back corner of the property over there by the row of copper birches, I created a huge butterfly garden. I think I was twenty or twenty-one and home from college at the time. It has beebalm, baptisia, yarrow, blazing star, lavender, calamintha, daisies, black-eyed susan, verbena, and buddleia. I set a cobblestone path through the middle with a few rustic, refurbished benches. It's one of Valerie's favorite places to get away."

It was hard to imagine what the backyard was like in the summer, but he hoped she could picture the magic.

"Behind the carriage house, Valerie and I built a patio and outdoor kitchen, complete with wood-fired pizza oven. In the west corner of the lawn, there are curved perennial beds, lined with limestone rocks. That one over there has several peony bushes that were our mother's babies. I built the rest of the flower beds around them. Do you see the rustic arbor back there, the one made of cedar logs?"

Sasha nodded, and Perry rested his hand on her hip.

"My granddad built that. It's covered in clematis and leads to a picnic area. I repurposed some of his old garden tools, along with antique farming equipment, into sculptures back behind it. You can't see them because they're covered in snow."

"So, you did all the landscaping back there?"

He shrugged. "It's hard to picture in the winter. Mostly, I added to what was already there. I love wild gardens that feel lived-in and natural. Gardening and landscaping aren't Valerie's forte. She hires someone to keep it in tip-top shape during the spring and summer."

Sasha turned and gazed up at him. "Why did you become an accountant, then?"

And wasn't that the million dollar question. He didn't want to go into his recent failings, not with a woman who seemed to know herself so well, who was so brave and interesting. He was the opposite of brave and interesting. He was an unemployed accountant who hadn't been interesting enough to keep his last girlfriend through his current job upheaval.

It paid to be self-aware.

"Pragmatism? Financial security?" he said with a laugh, but it wasn't funny. Being laid off and changing his career trajectory to a profession that was less financially solvent than accounting had not been a decision he'd made lightly. It had cost him so much.

"Pssh, life is too short not to take chances."

She squeezed his shoulder, and his chest ached with tenderness. He was trash at one-night stands. He felt way too much for her and way too soon.

"I'm kind of expecting everything to fall apart, more than it has at least. I haven't told Valerie that I lost my job, just that my ex and I broke up. She thinks I'm only here for Christmas. I'm nervous to ask her if I can stay. So I'm homeless, jobless, single, semi-directionless. I have a safety net, but that's about all I've got going for me right now."

He might as well have said that he was the opposite of a catch.

"As an older sister myself, I can tell you there isn't a single thing I wouldn't do for my younger brother. I'm sure Valerie feels the same way. I think you're brave. Leaving your home and stability and a relationship that wasn't working is scary. You have a big, romantic heart. That's a good thing."

He knew nothing of bravery, and he suspected he hadn't scratched the surface of the ways she outstripped him in that department.

"Thank you."

"What's your favorite flower?"

He caught her hand and laced their fingers together. She let him.

"This one. Peony." He tapped the huge tattoo on his side through his shirt.

"And your favorite Christmas plant?"

"Winterberry, of course. It gives the dreariness of winter a splash of color. There's a ton lining the front porch."

"I'm surprised it's not mistletoe," she said with a bit of cheek.

"Did you know mistletoe is a parasite?"

"*I did not.* How apt that it's associated with Christmas lovers, then."

He smiled. "Such a cynic."

"Guilty."

"Why do you hate Christmas?" he asked.

"Oh, hitting me with the tough questions."

She turned away from him and started wandering around the huge farmhouse table. In less than a week, this room would be decked out in hundreds of candles and full of Christmas lovers. The Soiree was quite the romantic event. He suddenly, desperately wished he'd get to share that with Sasha.

Fat chance.

"You don't have to tell me."

She shrugged. "In a nutshell—bad memories. And Christmas is inescapable. It's in every store, every business. There are whole radio stations dedicated to it. It's hard for me to stomach, that's all."

He suspected it went a lot deeper than that, but he wasn't going to push her.

"What about you? Why do you like Christmas?" she asked him.

"Well, it's part of my legacy, so there's that. Christmas has always been important to the inn. But other than that, maybe because it's romantic. I can sense possibility in the air, you know? Like there's hope and excitement and love all around, if I look close enough. It feels as if miracles can really happen." He shook his head. "That sounds corny."

"No. It's lovely. I'm glad there are people who aren't cynical and jaded about Christmas and romance and love. It's refreshing."

"I adore traditions too. Growing up, we'd go with our granddad to cut down Christmas trees for every room. He was very particular about picking each tree, and we got apple cider out of the deal. Valerie's been doing the tree shopping on her own for several years, but I think it's time to change that. There's also the Winterberry Christmas Couples' Soiree. It's a mini romantic Christmas getaway. Valerie and I used to spy on all the couples dancing and kissing and getting tipsy. I love thinking back on those traditions. They shaped me, for the better."

She picked at one of her fingernails, not meeting his eye. "That's nice. My siblings and I don't have any traditions, period, besides being obnoxious brunch rats."

"I wish——" He scratched his jaw. "I wish there was something I could do to make you like Christmas. Or to make this one better."

THIS WAS why Sasha didn't open up, why she didn't allow anyone in. She didn't want to hurt this beautiful, giving, romantic man, but she didn't trust in romance, or love, or relationships. Didn't want to put herself in a position to be smashed again.

He wanted to make her like Christmas again. That was impossible.

"Well, that orgasm has been the highlight so far," she said, pulling cheekiness over her like a costume. It worked, because it shattered the uncomfortable intimacy between them, and he took a step back.

A pained expression passed over his handsome face, and her stomach clenched. Resorting to sex and then diminishing the connection created by sex was probably her cruelest habit, but it also protected her.

This had gotten way too personal for Sasha's taste, so she left the formal dining room, pausing in a hallway to get her bearings. He followed her after a few seconds, appearing way more composed.

Perry made her feel safe. Safe to talk about her fears, her dreams, her goals, and she couldn't handle that. She wasn't sure what was causing it, what made him special. Maybe it was their circumstances—snowed-in at a cozy inn with a bag of sex toys to keep them busy. Or maybe it was because Christmas was only days away, and the spirit of the season was dimming her higher functioning brainpower, muddying her normal cynicism with festive happiness.

Yuck.

If life had taught her one thing, it was that the love and happiness surrounding Christmas was a total farce.

She was gearing up to retreat to her room, alone, when Valerie waltzed out of the kitchen with a plate of goodies and nearly tripped over Perry's feet.

"Oh, there you two are!" Valerie said. "I was about to send out a search party. You missed lunch."

The mention of food, as well as the aroma of pastry, hit Sasha like a big red sleigh. Her stomach growled loudly, and Valerie laughed.

"Here, try one of these. It's a goat cheese and fig tart with a honey glaze, and I have tea sandwiches in the kitchen."

Sasha gladly grabbed a tart and took a bite. The pastry was crispy and buttery, the goat cheese and fig filling heavenly. The honey complemented the sharpness of the goat cheese perfectly. She moaned as if the tart was the best thing she'd ever tasted.

It might have been. She wanted to fall at Valerie's feet in worship.

"Lead the way to the tea sandwiches, oh great temptress," Sasha said.

Valerie laughed, an evil glint in her eye. "Why don't you go on through to the breakfast room, and I'll bring them out?"

Sasha readily agreed but stopped in her tracks when she realized she'd been duped. The breakfast room was craft central. Everyone was lined up like little elves at the North Pole and surrounded by pinecones, ceramic figurines, winterberry swag, glitter, paint, glue, and all manner of other craft goods.

The ornament-making activity Valerie had been threatening … or, uh, advertising … this morning was in full swing.

So much glitter.

Damn it.

"You don't have to participate," Perry said in her ear when she faltered in the doorway. "I can snag you food and sneak it to your room?"

"Would you be joining me in said room?"

He smiled and shrugged. "Nah. I want to make some ornaments."

He probably needed a break from her and her whiplash.

Louise and Andie were sitting at one of the round tables and waved her over. The other person at the table with them was the emo teenager, who was painting a ceramic Christmas tree. His tree was matte black from top to bottom.

Ah, her kindred spirit, at it again.

With a roll of her shoulders, she joined them, Perry on her heels. Within seconds, Valerie plopped a plate of sandwiches and tarts in the middle of their table. It might be worth enduring craft time for the finger foods.

She grabbed a pinecone and a paintbrush. To the teenager, she said, "Can I borrow your screw-Christmas black paint?"

He grinned and passed it over.

Perry also grabbed a pinecone and paintbrush, as well as gold glitter. He'd undoubtedly paint the prettiest pinecone in all the land, and Sasha suddenly resented that.

She ripped into another fig and goat cheese tart, then gobbled up a salmon and caper salad tea sandwich on soda bread.

The atmosphere in the room was cozy and festive, everyone laughing and enjoying themselves, but Sasha couldn't fake it. She felt more separate from the happiness of the season than normal.

She was halfway done painting her pinecone black with hot pink seed tips when Andie interrupted her concentration.

"So, Sasha, how long have you been working in"—Andie threw a hasty glance at the teenage boy at their table, her eyes shining—"uh, sales?" Today Andie was wearing a chunky wool stocking cap over her short fro and bright purple lipstick that popped against her dark skin.

Sasha smiled. "I got my degree in marketing but started working at my current company after my best friend founded it seven years ago. She needed a marketing manager, so I stepped in. What do you do?"

"I'm getting my PhD in microbiology, but I also bartend a couple nights a week because the tips are stellar."

"I hear that," Sasha said. She'd waitressed in addition to her Lady Robin's Intimate Implements job until the company had exploded into success. "Where do you bartend?"

"It's a place in midtown called Rod's." Andie then mouthed, "*Strip club.*"

Sasha smiled and nodded. She knew of Rod's. It was a fancy, upscale place that had a women's night once a week where there were male dancers. She'd known a guy in college who had worked there. She imagined the tips were more than stellar considering the rich clientele.

"Did you ever think you'd be marketing the type of … umm …" Andie trailed off, obviously at a loss in how to describe sex toys in front of the teen boy, who didn't seem to be paying them any mind.

"Gizmos," Perry said, without glancing up from his pinecone. His ornament looked straight out of a West Elm catalog. He'd painted the seed tips dark green and was finishing them with golden glitter. It was the fanciest fucking pinecone Sasha had ever seen.

Andie laughed. "Yes, gizmos. Did you plan to go into gizmos? Or did you fall into it?"

Sasha shrugged. "Robin and I had been talking about it for years, almost as a joke. Then one day it stopped being a joke. I can't imagine doing anything else."

The teen boy glanced up then and grabbed a cucumber and cream cheese sandwich. "I don't know why you're all talking in circles." He pointed his sandwich at Sasha. "You sell sex toys." Then he turned to Andie. "And you work at the only strip club in the city that has male strippers."

Silence descended on the table until Sasha couldn't hold it in any longer. She burst into laughter.

"What's your name?" she asked him.

He blushed and flipped his black bangs out of his eyes. "Ryker."

"I think you're going places. How did you know what I sell?"

"I heard the laughter during the private party last night, so I snuck down to see what was going on. Kind of hard to miss the dildos being passed around."

"Oh geez." Sasha laughed into her hands. The whole table was trying to stifle their giggling.

"Highlight of this whole stupid family-bonding time," Ryker grumbled. "I hate Christmas."

"Why?" Andie asked him.

"My mom died around Christmas."

A hush of silence hit the table. Sasha glanced at the other tables that were occupied by Ryker's siblings. He was several years older than the next oldest, so they were probably half-siblings.

Perry tentatively said, "I'm really sorry. My dad died right before Thanksgiving when I was ten. It's hard to celebrate a holiday when a person you love is missing, isn't it?"

Ryker nodded. "Yes. *That*. But my dad and stepmom try to force it." He turned his attention back to his goth Christmas tree, where he'd started to paint tiny white skulls as ornaments.

Sasha's chest hurt suddenly, like someone had scooped her heart out with a spoon. She knew heartache, but she couldn't imagine losing a loving parent at such a young age. Neither of her parents had ever played a role in her life, and she couldn't say that she missed them much. But she did miss her grandmother every day, especially this time of year, when so many families came together to celebrate.

Sasha, Benji, and Rosie were their own support system now. Those first few years after their grandma had died, Sasha had overcompensated, feeling this need to keep her little family close and tied together. Basically, she'd become a Christmas nut.

Sasha had gone all in on Christmas, building it up as this uber-important holiday, giving it meaning that wasn't there. When P.J., her ex, had proposed, Sasha had pushed for a Christmas Eve wedding, thinking it would bring some of that specialness back to the season.

Instead, P.J. had left her at the altar and ruined Christmas for her for good.

Bile thickened in Sasha's throat, old hurts rushing up at her. She couldn't be here any longer. She needed out.

She started to stand as Valerie swept back into the room.

"Great news!" Valerie said loudly, so everyone could hear her. "Supposedly, there will be a bit of a break in the storm tomorrow morning. They're expecting the snow to slow down and the temperature to rise above thirty-two degrees for about four or five hours tomorrow before the second wave of storms hit us. It should be enough time for the interstate to open and for us to get a crew out here to clear the driveway. It looks like a jail break is imminent."

Sasha couldn't help herself—she glanced at Perry, and he was staring at her, sad shock on his face. She hadn't expected to get to go home tomorrow, and she should be ecstatic.

She *was* ecstatic!

Truly.

Mostly.

"That's awesome," Sasha said, her voice as measured as she could make it. "I think I'm going to try to catch a bit of a nap, if you'll excuse me."

She left her pinecone ornament on the table. It was too ugly for a tree anyway.

Chapter Six

*P*erry thought he'd escaped the crowd. Everyone else was playing Risk in the breakfast room or watching Christmas movies in the den, so he settled down with a book in front of the fire and nursed a beer.

It only took thirty minutes for his sister to find him.

"What's up, little bro?" she said as she melted into the chair next to him.

"Not much. Reading." He held up the old-school bodice ripper he'd nicked from her library in the attic.

Valerie laughed softly and leaned her head back. She had dark circles under her eyes. This whole snowed-in situation had to be stressful for her. She had several staff that helped run Winterberry Inn, but none of them had been able to make it out here in the storm. Also, the inn didn't usually have to feed its guests more than breakfast, but Valerie had been determined to make everyone's stay exceptional, even with a snow-pocalypse.

"How are you doing, Val?"

"Fine. I've got several pots of soup and chili going for dinner, as well as crusty bread. It'll be a nice, homey meal. Perfect snowed-in dinner."

"Sounds great. If you need anything, please ask me. I'm happy to help you." She didn't react, so he continued. "I can help with the Soiree too."

Valerie blew out a big breath, her cheeks puffing out, before she opened her eyes. "I'm a bit behind on that actually."

"You always are," Perry teased. It was a large, extravagant party. Not an easy thing to plan on your own. "What do you need help with?"

"The decorations mostly, which you'll be awesome at. Eden is in charge of the menu, so no worries for me there. But transforming the inn into a romantic winter wonderland is a tad stressful. So many candles. Normally, I'd be setting up already, but with all the guests stranded here, I decided to wait."

"Makes sense. Once the storm passes, we'll hit the prepping hard."

Valerie smiled and stole his beer from his fingers. "I'm so happy you're here. I wish you lived closer, then you could help me all the time." He started to open his mouth, to dump his truth on her, but she didn't give him a chance to break in. "Man, if you lived here, you could try for something real with Sasha. You guys are adorably awkward around each other. And don't lie. I know you've been getting up to some hanky-panky, Mr. Disappeared-With-The-Sex-Toy-Lady all afternoon."

Perry laughed uncomfortably. "So, I have a lot of things to tell you, but I don't know where to start."

"Start with which sex toys you've used."

"Ew, no. I'm not giving you details. And tomorrow, she'll go back to her exciting, interesting life and forget about boring ol' me."

Perry jerked when Valerie punched his arm. "Stop the pity party. It looks ridiculous on you."

He smiled at his sister. She knew exactly how to break him out of his moods.

"So I told you Brit and I broke up earlier this month." he said.

Valerie nodded, her brows furrowing down. His ex-girlfriend and Valerie had never exactly gotten along, which should have been a warning signal. He was obviously good at ignoring his gut instinct when it came to his life, though. He'd done it with his accounting job for almost eight years.

"Well, we broke up because I got laid off and then decided to use my severance package to go back to school."

"Oh, thank God."

Perry gaped at her. "What?"

"You were miserable in that job, but it's like you thought that hating your job was part of being an adult. If that's true, then I don't want to grow up. What do you want to do instead?"

This conversation was not going how he'd expected. "I enrolled in the horticulture and landscape architecture program. Here. In the city."

"Shut the fuck up! You're moving here?"

"My car is full of my shit. I sold my furniture."

Valerie hugged him. "My little brother is back. Oh my God, I'm so happy. Best. Christmas. Ever."

Perry laughed. "Do you think I'm making a mistake?"

She leaned back. "Absolutely not. You'll be so great at that. I'm asked all the time who did our landscaping! I'm excited for you."

"Thanks, Val. I'm nervous. I'm essentially jobless and homeless right now."

"You're not homeless. Hell, you can stay in the Red Cedar Room for a while. I can mark it as booked for the foreseeable future. Or you can move into your childhood bedroom in the carriage house."

They both laughed. Once Valerie had taken over the Winterberry Inn, she'd also renovated the carriage house. It didn't resemble their childhood home in the least, but it reflected her farmhouse-chic style. His childhood bedroom was her quilting room.

"I'm happy I'm here," he said and stole his beer back.

"Maybe …" Valerie glanced at him and frowned. "Never mind."

"What?"

"I was scheming."

"About what?"

"Matchmaking."

Perry turned in his seat to face her. "Valerie, no. Whatever you're planning—don't."

"I'm just saying … we host the 'most romantic Christmas party in the Midwest' according to *Midwestern*

Living. It'd be the perfect party to invite someone's new fuck buddy to."

"That's not a good idea. She's made it pretty clear she doesn't do romance. Or Christmas."

"Maybe she simply needs the right person to bust her out of her shell?" Valerie said.

"Maybe you've been reading too many romance novels?"

Valerie tapped the old romance in his hand. "You too, brother. Anything can happen at Christmas. Isn't that the magic of the season? People open their hearts and miracles happen."

"Sasha agreeing to come with me to the Soiree is about as likely as a flying reindeer."

"If you don't believe, you won't receive, Perry."

He laughed. "Oh, fuck off."

"Fine." She lightly kissed his cheek after standing up. "I love you."

"Love you too."

"But you still owe me a 2013 Venge Vineyard Late Harvest Zinfandel."

"Shit. Sorry," he called after her as she waltzed out of the room, throwing a cheeky smile over her shoulder.

He stared down at the cover of the romance he'd been reading. It showed a couple in a sensual clench, both partially undressed and seemingly wrapped up in each other.

Maybe one day he'd have that, but it wouldn't be with Sasha. Hell, right now, with his life in total upheaval, it was undoubtedly the worst time to fall for someone, but he was.

Falling.

He wouldn't push Sasha. There were a million reasons Sasha might not want a relationship. Even more reasons not to want one with him. It wasn't his place to try to change her mind. Part of his heart, his mind, was screaming at him to fight it, to help her see that they could be great together. But he respected her too much.

He'd read one too many romance novels if he thought two days of sex with an unemployed accountant was going to change her mind. He returned to his book.

Dinner snuck up on him a few hours later. He was half-asleep next to the fire when Andie and Karen found him.

"Hey, lover boy. Time to eat," Karen said after snapping next to his ear. "Your sister made chili. She says it's spicy, but I don't trust that girl to know her way around spicy." Both Andie and Karen laughed at that, and Perry stretched.

"It won't be spicy. She's a weenie."

"Figures. Why so glum?" Karen asked. Perry had known Karen for over five years, and he recognized the sudden seriousness in her voice. She'd always been able to get the young members of the Staunchly Raunchy Book Club to open up when they needed to. She'd probably been trained in interrogation.

Andie patted Perry's shoulder and left the room, giving them space.

"I'm fine," he said, wishing it were true.

"Sure you are." The sarcasm pitched Karen's voice deeper. "Does this have to do with Ms. Sasha Holiday?"

He shrugged and tried to put on a relaxed smile. "I'm fine. Promise. I barely know Sasha."

"Sometimes we just know that it's special. I'd never been with a woman until I met Andie."

"Really?"

"I was with Devon for over twenty years, and I miss him every day, especially this time of year." Perry nodded, recognizing the name of Karen's late husband. She smiled. "When I met Andie, I knew immediately that we were meant to be, that we would be incredible together, but I was scared and mourning. So I moved slow. And she let me. She let me take my time, get my bearings. I'm so thankful for that."

"That's a beautiful story."

"Do you get what I'm trying to tell you, hon?"

"Not exactly." He tugged on his hair, trying to wake himself up.

"Sasha lit up like a Christmas tree when you first walked in the other night. She can't keep her eyes off you. And you're the same. Maybe it's only sex. Maybe it's attraction that will fizzle out. But I think it's more, and I'm pretty fucking smart."

Perry's stomach clenched. "I wish it was more, but she doesn't want that."

"And I'm saying, let her be scared. Give her time to get her bearings. Give her space to figure it out. Maybe she won't come to her senses, but maybe she will."

"I don't want to get hurt."

"Oh, sweetheart, I don't want that for you, either." Karen reached over and squeezed his knee. "Sometimes love is a risk. The best kind of risk, and you deserve all the love."

He smiled at her as a sudden jingle of bells sounded behind them. He turned in his chair to see Sasha, wearing her reindeer antlers again, walking out of the room.

I DON'T WANT to get hurt.

I don't want to get hurt.

Those words rang through Sasha's ears through dinner. She'd donned the stupid-ass reindeer antlers and a Christmas sweatshirt from Valerie in the hopes that a little cheer would do her some good. She'd fake it to make it and all that crap.

After the talk with Ryker earlier, she'd decided it was worth it to pull on false merriness like an ill-fitting Santa costume this evening. She only needed to make it through a few more hours of cozy Christmas social time, then she was home free come morning.

And yeah, the thought of leaving tomorrow left her breathless and hurting, a physical ache from her ribs to the pit of her stomach. She'd never see Andie and Karen, who were the biggest troublemakers ever. Never see Louise, who was sweet and shy, or Valerie, who could so easily become a friend.

And she'd never see Perry Winters.

She kept trying to convince herself that they could

somehow continue this no-strings affair, that it didn't mean anything and they were on the same page, so it was okay to keep seeing each other once the storm passed. But she couldn't lie anymore.

I don't want to get hurt.

She didn't want to hurt him. Their goals, their hopes were too incompatible. He deserved a woman who would cuddle up to him while roasting chestnuts in the fire or who would help him trim the million Christmas trees in this adorable bed and breakfast.

He deserved a partner who would happily dance with him at the Winterberry Sappy Christmas Twosomes' Extravaganza or whatever it was called. And that would never be her.

She was almost sure it could never be her.

"More butternut squash soup, Sasha?" Valerie asked her, snapping her out of it. "Or maybe chili?"

"I'll try the chili. The butternut squash was amazing, though." Everything Valerie had fed her had been exceptional. No wonder this place was so successful.

It tasted of home.

If you had a fancy pastry chef at home.

Valerie ladled her some chili, and Perry passed her a dish of fixings.

Sasha dug into her chili after crushing crackers on the top and garnishing it with sour cream and shredded cheese. The chili was meaty with a rich, hearty tomato sauce and an underlying bite of heat. The sour cream lent it a cool smoothness.

"Valerie, will you marry me? Shit, this is delicious," Sasha said after downing half her bowl.

Everyone laughed, and Sasha caught Perry's eye. He was grinning at her, which made her blush for some ungodly reason.

"Valerie eats microwave meals every night," Louise said, a hint of teasing in her voice. "She says she doesn't like to take work home with her."

Valerie plopped down next to Louise and leaned her head on her shoulder playfully. "I just need a good woman to cook for."

Louise bit her lip and a secret smile stretched over her face. Sasha couldn't watch their awkward, tentative courtship. It made something in her chest flutter, like a bunch of calling birds finally finding their wings.

Sasha quickly finished her chili and got up to clean her bowl and plate. Perry followed her.

"Are you okay?" he asked as he rinsed their bowls in the kitchen sink.

"Yep." She tried to sound casual, even though she really didn't feel *okay* at all.

Christmas sucked.

Love and mushiness sucked.

She suddenly wished she was in her own bed and her own anti-Christmas apartment with a fierceness that nearly brought her to her knees.

"Valerie thawed a package of chestnuts she bought at the farmers market. Want to help me prepare them? We're going to roast them in the fireplace once everyone is done with dinner."

Of course. Chestnuts on an open fire. This place was a ridiculous fairy tale.

"Sure. What do you need me to do?"

"We need to wash and score the shells with an x."

"Hand me a knife then."

Perry smiled and kissed her gingerly, barely a brush of lips.

"What was that for?" she asked.

"No reason. I wanted to, is all."

She shot him a silly, narrow-eyed glare. "You behave."

"Aye, aye."

They worked in companionable silence for several minutes, Perry rinsing the chestnuts and Sasha scoring them. Once they were washed, Perry picked up his own knife and they finished the job.

Perry dumped the chestnuts into a large chestnut roaster. It resembled a long-handled popcorn popper. Who actually owned a designated chestnut roaster?

A Christmas-themed inn, evidently.

She followed him into the hearth room, where most of the guests had gathered.

With gentle hands, Perry placed the roaster into the fire. Then he grabbed a deep-red afghan and a large cushion from a basket by the sofa. There were no empty seats.

"Here. Get comfy," he said to Sasha, building her a nest close to the fire. "I'll get us drinks. What would you like? Wine, beer, hot chocolate, apple cider, eggnog?"

"Apple cider."

He smiled. "You got it."

When he returned, two mugs of hot cider in hand, both garnished with a cinnamon stick and slices of blood orange like something straight out of a Pinterest post, she couldn't hold in her smile. Damn these people and their Christmas spirit. At least she was getting incredible food out of this nightmare.

Perry settled onto the floor next to her, close enough to the hearth that he could shake the chestnut roaster every few minutes. Everything was so warm—her hands wrapped around a mug of the most magical cider in the history of the world, her toes that were close to the fire, her body wrapped in a chunky blanket. Her cheeks that were full-on blushing as Perry scooted closer to her.

Oh, geez. They were cuddling in front of a fireplace while chestnuts roasted over an open flame, sizzling and popping and sending sweet nutty smells through the room. The whole scene was picture perfect. She wanted to lean back into his body but couldn't allow herself that type of pleasure. It was ephemeral. It wouldn't last. She wouldn't let it.

Perry got up on his knees to shake the chestnut roaster again, and she checked him out. He was still in gray sweats and a soft, flannel shirt. The sweatpants framed his firm, round butt. She wanted to smack it.

The thought made her laugh and a different kind of warmth bubble up in her. He settled back down beside her.

She leaned into him and put her mouth against the shell of his ear. "You have a rocking ass. Has anyone ever told you that?" she whispered.

Rosiness spread over the apples of his cheeks. He shook his head and bit his bottom lip on a grin.

"Your other attributes aren't half bad either."

"Good to know," he whispered back. "Your butt is pretty spectacular too. I want to do all kinds of things to it."

She felt as if they were in their own world. Everyone else was chattering away, leaving them alone.

It was easier to flirt and talk about sex than emotions. Easier to let herself get carried away with Perry's unbearable sexiness than to confront the fact that he made her heart clench and stutter for a million reasons that had nothing to do with fucking.

"I'd let you," she said.

"Would you now?"

"I think I've proven I am totally down, Perry."

He bumped his shoulder against hers. "And what else do you have in that Santa's big red bag of debauchery? Anything that might prove helpful?"

"Ho, ho, ho." She winked.

He laughed loudly, genuine joy etched in every line of his face. His laughter drew glances from a few people around the room.

Sasha took a hasty sip of cider to hide her own delight. She let happiness rush through her. One more night of this.

She'd allow herself one more night of this.

Soon, the chestnuts were done and Perry pulled them off the fire. Valerie passed him two bowls, and after letting them cool, he started peeling them, discarding the shells and skin into one bowl and the meaty nut into another that was full of cinnamon sugar. Perry and Valerie moved around each other through this process seamlessly.

Perry parceled some of the treat into a little bowl for him and Sasha.

He lifted up the bowl. "Okay, Sasha. You ready to try these nuts?"

Chapter Seven

*S*asha fell back onto Perry's bed, her stomach full of laughter. Perry kneeled next to her and popped a chestnut past her lips. She nipped his fingers lightly, then chewed the sweet nut.

She'd never had chestnuts before, and she had no idea if they were always so amazing or if it was because Perry was feeding them to her.

He followed his fingers with his lips, kissing her mouth, her chin, down to her throat before sitting up and eating a chestnut of his own.

They'd managed to socialize with the other Winter-berry guests for about twenty minutes. Twenty minutes of feverish, festive eye-fucking. Now, they finished their bowl of chestnuts, sharing kisses and laughter over nothing at all.

Perry's room was similar to hers, except it was on the corner of the house, so it had double the windows. His canopy bed had rainbow-colored Christmas lights wrapped around the posts. The Christmas tree in the corner of his room was huge with thick branches full of spindly needles. His whole room smelled of clean, bitter evergreen, and his skin smelled like smoky cedar.

The Fancy Fleshstroker and her black silky thong were on top of an antique dresser, and they stood out among the twee decorations, glaring in their filthiness.

Perry's mouth landed on the edge of her jaw, and she tipped her head back, gasping.

"We need my roller bag."

"The one full of Christmas miracles?" he asked, smiling against her neck.

"That's the ticket."

"I'll get it." He jumped up off the bed and jogged into the adjoining bathroom and, she assumed, into the Blue Spruce Room. He came back seconds later with her Lady Robin's roller bag in hand, a huge grin on his face.

Her heart tumbled over, like a snowball falling down a hill, gaining momentum, faster and faster. Hopefully, it wouldn't hit the bottom and explode into nothing but powder. "I'm leaving tomorrow."

His smile faltered for half a second, then he shrugged. "I know."

"And you're okay with that?"

She wasn't sure she could say the words outright, couldn't ask him if he was okay sleeping with her for one last night when it wouldn't lead to anything. But how ridiculous was she? If she couldn't hear the words out loud, then she shouldn't be living by that philosophy.

She took a deep breath. "Are you okay with one more night of no-strings-attached sex?"

His lips quirked. "On the second day of Christmas my fuck buddy gave to me?" he said, his voice musical but gruff.

"The screw of your life, baby. Get over here."

Perry lifted her red bag of toys onto the bed beside her, and she methodically pulled out the stock that she hadn't sold and the stock she'd used as samples for the party, meaning they had already been charged.

The Rimmy. P-spot Pulse and Pulse 2. Collar Me Nipple Clamps. Sporty Strap-on with Diamond Glass Dildo. Monster Me Tentacle Dildo. Monster Me Mermaid Dildo. Fingerslip Vibrator. Not Your Mother's Pearls Anal Beads. The Shake and Shimmy Cock Ring. The Slim and Simple Vibrator Wand.

"We also have your Fancy Fleshstroker, the Double Trouble, the Rude Beast, and the Chained Melody Clamps, all of which we've already used," she said.

Perry stared at the array of silicone and metal and glass with eyes as wide as saucers. He smiled like a kid on Christmas morning getting the first look at his loot.

"Pick your poison, Perry."

She'd been excited for the sweet holiday bonus that she'd earned from the Staunchly Raunchy Book Club Party, but at the rate she and Perry were going, she'd be lucky to break even after she expensed the toys they'd broken into.

And she couldn't have been happier about that fact.

"Anything here off limits? Anything you don't enjoy?" Perry asked.

She grinned, happy he'd thought to ask. "The Monster Me Dildos are a bit much for me. Fun when I want sex to feel like a freak show, but that's not what I'm interested in tonight. Everything else is fair game."

He nodded and selected the Rimmy, the Fingerslip, and the Shake and Shimmy Cock Ring. She was happy with his choices. They were all fairly non-invasive or discreet sex toys, and they suited what she knew of him. She liked that he wasn't pushing himself too far out of his comfort zone while still taking a walk on the wild side with her.

She pulled out the bottle of lube they'd already opened and some Lady Robin's antibacterial toy-cleaning wipes. She quickly threw the extra toys back into the bag and cleaned the ones he'd selected. All in all, it took under two minutes, but she felt self-conscious about the time wasted.

"So how are we doing this?" she asked as she stripped off her sweatshirt and unclipped her bra. Heat darkened his hazel eyes. She tossed her bra at him with a laugh. He caught it and brought it to his nose to smell.

God, he really was a dirty fucker and didn't even seem to realize it. First, he'd sucked her arousal off that dildo this afternoon, now he was sniffing her intimates. She liked that he kept surprising her.

He took off his clothes with a single-minded determination, then grabbed her legs and yanked her to the center of the bed, dragging her sweatpants off.

"I'm going to take you apart bit by bit," he said.

"Oh. Okay." She sent him an ornery smile.

"You don't believe me?"

She laughed. "No, I actually do. I'm just a brat."

"I love that about you," he said as he slid the Finger-slip over his index finger. Then he grabbed the Rimmy and flipped her onto her stomach.

Her head spun. She watched over her shoulder as Perry spread lube on the toy, then turned it on. It didn't exactly have vibration, but instead, tiny beads rotated around the stem of the plug.

"Can I use this on you?" he asked her. "Do you want it?"

"God, yes. Please."

With a rough tug, he brought her up onto her knees and spread her legs wide, exposing her. He touched the Rimmy to her asshole, and she breathed out slowly. The lube was slick but not messy, and she could take the toy easily. She knew from experience.

She also knew that it would make her legs shake and uncontrollable noises fall from her lips.

Perry pressed it in slowly but surely and within seconds it was seated. The rotating beads were meant to feel like rimming, and she groaned at the onslaught. The Rimmy was small but sent a delicious stretch through her. Her legs trembled, and she gasped through the sudden, silky pleasure.

God, how that must look to him? It made her stomach flutter. The end of the Rimmy was metal and shiny, and it had to be peeking up through her cheeks, giving him quite the show.

"You're beautiful," he said unevenly. He shouldered her legs further apart, then leaned down and licked her clit. His nose rubbed through the folds of her pussy.

She cried out, surprised by his mouth. He sucked on her clit before pulling the plug out slightly and gently pushing it back in. He kept this up for several minutes, a nice slow thrusting of the Rimmy and intense suction on her clit.

She squirmed against his mouth, unable to stay still, as he devoured her. She felt the slickness of her arousal dripping down her thighs and the wetness of the toy as it slipped in and out of her.

"Perry. This is … You're so … Oh, holy hell."

He tossed her onto her back with a sexy, fucking growl. The abrupt movement made the Rimmy press and shift inside her, which punched her excitement up another notch.

While hovering over her between her legs, Perry snuck his finger, equipped with the vibrating Fingerslip, into her cunt and touched her G-spot lightly, the vibration enough to make her back bow off the bed. His mouth found her again, the rough scratch of his beard lighting up her sensitive flesh. Everything was wet and slippery.

"You have such good hand-mouth coordination," she said, her voice strained and faint.

He chuckled against her, his lips humming against her clit. She fisted his hair.

Her orgasm slammed into her like a train thundering

down the tracks, whistle blowing. Her body clenched and pulsed around his finger, around the plug.

All she could see were Christmas colors and lights and the blood red of Perry's mouth as he lifted his lips away from her.

His beard was wet.

Damn, she could get used to that sight.

PERRY SUCKED the taste of Sasha off his lips.

So fucking perfect.

She was shaking, coming down from her orgasm, an almost pained expression on her face, her eyebrows pinched and her bottom lip between her teeth.

"You okay, beautiful?" he asked.

"Yeah." Her voice was breathy and strained. "I'm still, you know, *fuck*." She gestured down to where his finger, wearing the nifty Fingerslip, was lodged between her pussy lips. The Rimmy was happily working its magic too. She tipped her head back, exposing the gorgeous long length of her neck.

"Feeling it?"

She nodded on a gasp.

God, he wanted her. Wanted to be inside her in every way possible. Wanted her to be so overwhelmed with sensation that she screamed and held him close and kissed him like he was her only source of oxygen.

He pulled his finger out of her but left the Rimmy. He nudged it gently. "Do I need to take this out?"

She shook her head. "It's good. Really good."

He grinned. "Umm, can we? Do you want …" He sighed as reality came crashing down. "I don't have any condoms with me. Not that you'd want to have sex. But if you did. I don't have condoms, so we can't. God, I'll shut up now." He hid his face against her thigh, pressing the heat of his blush into her skin.

She laughed. "I do want that. There's some in the front pocket of my toy bag," she said, with a wave toward her roller bag. He crawled out of bed and found a rubber right where she'd said.

These small roadblocks, the logistics of sex, had always tripped him up and made him self-conscious, but Sasha watched his movements with thinly veiled need.

When he was back between her thighs, he thrust two digits into her, catching her slickness on his fingertips. Her warmth, her wetness, the sight of her spread in front of him—it all coalesced in his chest, made him shake from his desire to get inside her, to make her need as sharp and overwhelming as his. He fucked her with his fingers shallowly, and with his other hand, he thrummed his index finger, sheathed in the Fingerslip, over her clit. He wished he had a third hand available to play with the Rimmy too, but, alas, he was not so equipped. He loved the fact that it had been going the whole time, giving her constant stimulation.

The tension in her came on in bits and pieces. First the curling of her toes, then the arch of her feet. Next, her hands fisting the sheets. And finally, she tensed up at the waist, her shoulder blades leaving the bed. He pinched her clit between his index finger and thumb, and she thrashed.

"Perry, *oh God.*"

That tension snapped and her cunt pulsed around his fingers. She moaned low in her throat—a sexy, tortured sound—and her body shook from the force of her climax.

When her back hit the bed again, he pulled out his fingers and sucked her juices off them. He could die happy with her taste on his lips.

"You ready for this?" Sasha said, her voice cracking. She held up the Shimmy and Shake Cock Ring. "You need to put it on before you're fully hard."

"I've never used one."

"Yup. All right." She shook her head, like she was trying to clear the cotton from it, obviously not fully recovered from her two orgasms yet. Then she spread lube around the inside of the smooth silicone ring. It had a ridged oval on the top that he'd assumed was a clitoral vibrator, but she adjusted the oval so it faced down as she slid the ring behind his balls and up over his shaft. The oval was nestled against his perineum.

She glanced up at him. "You okay? Does it hurt at all? Tell the truth."

His cock quickly stiffened, the veins prominent. It felt different but not bad. Just intense. "No. It's good."

"Great." She pressed a little button next to the oval to turn the vibration on. It created a soft pulsing against the back of his balls and sent a rush of fire to his head. "What about now? Still okay?"

"Uh-huh." He was better than okay. He could hardly form words.

Next he skinned on a condom and dribbled lube over his cock. She stared, eyes hungry again. He held up the Fingerslip. "Trade?"

"Okay." Her voice was breathy.

With a smile, he took the Fingerslip off his hand and tenderly placed it onto her index finger.

"Remember when you asked me if I'd heard of the orgasm gap?" He grabbed her by the hips and flipped her over onto her hands and knees. "This okay?"

"*Yes.*" She went down onto her elbows, her head hanging. He spread her ass cheeks, and she made a vulnerable, hitching sound. Her body was gorgeous. Everything about it. He nudged the Rimmy, and she shivered hard.

"I want to … Can I take this out?" he asked, with another nudge against the sex toy. He wanted to see all of her. She nodded, so he gently pulled the Rimmy free.

He lightly traced her asshole with his thumb, trying to touch every part of her, learn her, experience as much as he could before this ended.

"I know about the orgasm gap because of romance novels," he continued. He pressed the head of his slick cock between the lips of her pussy, and it was so warm and so soft that he couldn't help but push in another inch. The sensation on his dick was incredible, more powerful than usual, like his skin was extra sensitive.

They both sucked in greedy, lusty breaths at the same time.

Through gritted teeth, he said, "Heroines in romance novels normally have double the orgasms of the heroes. It's a reversal of the orgasm gap in real life. I love that about romance novels. One of my favorite things."

He thrust deeper, and her back bowed, the deep ditch of her spine a beautiful, bright line.

"Am I going to be able to help you come again, Sasha?" he asked. A blush was spreading across her back, and he was sure it would be vibrant on her breasts and face, if he were to turn her over.

"Yeah, probably," she said breathlessly. "The lube was a good choice."

He laughed. Everything was wet and smooth. He rolled his hips into her, shafting deeper. Each thrust in felt like the first one, and the vibration behind his balls had him panting already. He couldn't help but grab the meaty flesh of her ass. She had thin silvery-white stretch marks on her hips, extending onto her butt cheeks. So fucking sexy. Pleasure curled in the base of his spine, like a tight, hot coil of need.

He touched her asshole again, and her whole body shook, her hips lifting up toward him. His hand was still a little slick from the lube but not slick enough.

"Sasha, can I?" He tapped his thumb against her hole lightly and thrust his cock into her pussy harder.

"*God, yes*. Fill me up." Her voice was wrecked, shot.

The bottle of lube had landed somewhere by his knee and he found it again, dribbling it over her crack. When she was slick, he pressed his thumb inside her ass, gripping her round cheek with his fingers. She was so hot and tight inside. It made his head spin.

Her body went rigid, and words poured from her, like a damn had broken. "So ... oh fuck, Perry. More, please. I want ... You feel incredible."

He slowed the roll of his hips, which made her wilder. She bucked against him, and her elbows collapsed out from under her until her chest was flat against the bed.

She reached underneath herself, putting the Fingerslip to use. He could feel the vibration from the toy moving through her. It made his eyes roll back, and he had to grip her side with his free hand so he didn't collapse on her. He stroked up her ribs and over her shoulder with one hand and rolled his thumb in her ass with his other.

"Such a good ... multitasker," she said, gasping and trembling.

He tried to laugh, but it came out as a hungry moan. He knew, without a doubt, that if not for the cock ring, he'd have come at that first press of his thumb into her ass.

His heart thundered in his ears, his body spurring him on to dive into her body, to drench himself in this perfect pleasure. To take and give as much as possible.

He could see her profile, and her cheeks were flushed a Christmas red. Her hair was damp from sweat, and she seemed incapable of any words, any noise, besides sweet, broken cries.

He couldn't believe he was inside her like this. Inside

her in two places—his cock in the smooth, wet warmth of her pussy, his thumb in her amazing ass. She quaked as he pushed his thumb slightly deeper. Her body tightened everywhere.

"Come on, beautiful," he whispered.

"*Perry!*"

She came again, wrenching and violent, this time with his name on her lips. He had to grind his teeth against the onslaught of his own pleasure, to hold it back, as her body throbbed around him.

He held himself still as a statue through her orgasm, just to absorb it. To live in this reality for a moment longer. As the tension soaked from her body, he pulled out of her ass and her sweet pussy and gently turned her over.

"Are you okay?" he asked.

She looked wrecked, her arms splayed to the sides, her eyes closed.

"*Yes.*"

She wrapped her legs around his waist, her thighs silky against him, and he entered her again. He kissed the rosy, tender tips of her nipples and the undersides of her breasts before mouthing up to her throat.

She gazed up at him. "Are *you* okay?"

"Yes. Want to see you." *Want you to see me.*

Staring down at her, their bodies so close, him completely covering her—this felt more intimate than anything else they'd done. His chest ached suddenly, and he kissed her lips.

They found a slow, intense rhythm. One that lit his blood on fire, made him feel vulnerable and exposed.

He worshiped her body with his, and she twisted her arms around him, tugging him closer. They were pressed together everywhere, her soft body accepting him.

A rush of heat spiked through him, and he drove into her harder. She grabbed his face and gazed straight up into his eyes.

His orgasm began as if in slow motion but harsher than ever before. Like it was being yanked out of him slowly, roughly. His balls tightened and clenched, the vibration on his taint causing all the blood in his body to throb. His ears and eyes, his tongue, his fingertips—they all pulsed in time to the slow spirals of his orgasm.

"*Oh holy night.* Fuck," he said.

Sasha laughed, her face transforming with joy. And that laugh, that absolute elation on her face, was what ripped him apart for good.

SASHA'S ABILITY TO keep this beautiful man behind his proper barrier had completely melted the moment he'd made her come. *Multiple times.* It wasn't the first time she'd had great sex. It wasn't the first time *this month* she'd had great sex, but Perry was different. Had been from the moment he'd startled her into dropping the P-Spot Pulse onto that hardwood floor.

All the tension, all the suspicion she normally armed

her heart with, had leeched from her, and she wasn't strong enough to build it back up at the moment.

His hand was running a circuit over her hip and thigh, the steady thump of his heart sounding in her ear. It was cozy.

And awful.

Well, okay, it was kind of wonderful because Perry was kind of wonderful. And she resented it.

"Are you cold?" he asked her, his voice languid and lazy, like their sex had made him soft and fuzzy around the edges.

"A bit."

After Perry had come, he'd dispensed with the condom and sex toys, then cleaned them both up with a wet washrag. But now the remnants of water on her body were giving her the chills. He leaned over the side of his bed and grabbed his thick flannel shirt. She greedily snatched it from his hands and slipped it on, buttoning it up halfway.

He started to roll out of bed. "Let me grab your sweats too."

"No, I'm fine. This will be enough."

She lifted the cuff to her nose and inhaled. The fabric held a hint of his scent—that woodsy, earthy smell she wanted to bathe in.

"You have no idea how fucking sexy you look right now."

Sasha glanced up from her horny shirt-sniffing. "Huh?"

He smiled and shook his head. "Wearing my shirt. No

panties or pants. Your hair wild and spiky with sweat. Your lips red from my kisses." He crawled over her and pressed his mouth to hers. "So fucking sexy."

She stroked her hands down his back all the way to his tight butt, which she grabbed because it was a nice butt that deserved some love.

"Back atcha."

He lifted his face so he could grin at her, and her breath tumbled in her lungs. He was more than sexy. Perry was beautiful. So fun and expressive and open.

She wished … well, she wished she were different. Wished she could be what he needed.

I don't want to get hurt.

The last thing Sasha wanted was to hurt him. Or get hurt herself. Maybe she should get out of his bed, out of his room, away from all the sparkly Christmas lights and warm feelings.

But she couldn't. Not yet.

Perry rolled off her and cuddled her against him, their limbs tangling together, her cheek back on his chest.

The silence between them grew oppressive—not because it was uncomfortable but because it was the opposite. She could have happily laid in his arms, wearing his flannel shirt and listening to him breathe for the entire night. But that very fact scared her shitless.

"So you and your ex just broke up?" she said, because there was nothing quite so awkward as talking about exes while naked in bed together. It would make anyone's asshole clench.

He snorted and pressed his forehead into the space

between her neck and shoulder. "Yes. At the beginning of December."

"Well, you needed a rebound then."

His body stilled, like she'd paused a videogame, before he took a deep, halting breath. "I guess so." He propped himself up on an elbow. "Do you think rebounds really work?"

"For some people." They had never worked for her, though. "A rebound fuck can help someone move on or make them miss the other person. It can give a person the confidence to get back out there in the dating game of life. Or it can show them that they're not ready yet. I guess it depends on how you view sex and why you do it."

"I didn't think of this as a rebound when we started. I simply knew I wanted you, wanted to get to know you. I'm happy I did."

"I'm happy you did too."

Talk about an understatement. He made her fucking fly.

"How do you view sex?" he asked. "You said rebounds depend 'on how you view sex.' What do you mean?"

"I guess I mean whether it's a big emotional schmaltzy experience for you or if it's a fun release of tension. Both are good."

She pictured his eyes before he'd come. The way they'd widened, the vulnerable hitch of his eyebrows, as if he was in some kind of emotional pain. She'd needed to touch him, to feel it—his emotions, his release.

As hot as the whole experience had been, it had also

struck her heart like an arrow. She'd felt it to her very core. Their connection, the intimacy.

"Right. But what is it to you? Are you telling me emotions are never involved?" Perry's voice wavered with hurt.

"Of course not. I don't sleep with people I don't like and enjoy, so there are always emotions there. Fondness, tenderness. But I don't allow myself to get attached."

Considering she was thinking about stealing Perry's flannel, that was a big-ass lie. She was more than attached, but she wasn't brave enough to face what that meant.

Letting him in for a few days, over the course of a snowstorm, was very different than opening up completely. And that was what a relationship was—the breakdown of every barrier and wall she'd built up around her heart as protection.

She wasn't sure she was ready to do that yet. Or if she ever would be again.

PERRY WANTED to make her see that they could fit together, that he was worth the trouble.

It would be a Christmas miracle if she agreed.

He was taking control of his life. He'd left a career that he didn't enjoy, enrolled in school, moved back home. And part of him wanted to try to take control of this situation too. To bully Sasha into seeing how wonderful they could be together.

But he wasn't a bully. He was easygoing and loved romance novels. He wasn't going to use the vulnerability of the moment to try to convince Sasha to change her mind about relationships. She was adamant, and he respected her.

So instead, he kissed her until she was relaxed in his arms. He was going to enjoy these last moments with her before she drove off in the morning and he never saw her again.

She traced her fingertips over his tattoos, and he rubbed his hands over her long legs and back. They touched and kissed for ages, the only light in the room coming from the Christmas lights.

It was beautiful. Sasha looked like a festive lumberjack in his red and green flannel shirt. The room smelled of sex and pine needles. It was a filthy Christmas fairy tale.

He never wanted this moment to end, so he fought sleep like the devil.

"I'm so glad I met you," he said, as her eyes began to close and her legs went heavy against him.

She smiled slightly, her full lips quirking at the corners. "I'm glad I met you too. I wish I were different, Perry. I really do."

His heartbeat seemed to freeze in his chest before taking off at double-time. "What do you mean?"

"You're taking advantage of my sleepiness." She leaned in and kissed him below his Adam's apple.

"Guilty," he said, running his hands through her hair. "You don't have to tell me."

She huffed and snuggled closer. "I never had big family Christmases as a kid. We did a couple presents and a fake tree and then frozen pizza. As an adult, I was determined to change that. I wanted to have the big Christmas dinners with the beautiful decorations and all the wonderful traditions."

"That makes sense." He caressed her cheekbone and tried to brace himself. He was sure she was about to drop a bombshell on him. The hurt in her eyes was killing him.

"What better way to make Christmas special than a Christmas wedding."

"Oh no."

Sasha laughed wryly and pushed into his hand. "I was left at the altar on Christmas Eve last year. He just didn't show up. I'd planned this big holiday-themed spectacular. Everything was red and green and glittery. I threw my heart and soul into making this beautiful winter wedding. It was going to be festive, and happy, and *perfect*. His best man broke the news to me right after I'd put on my wedding dress."

"What an asshole."

Her eyes got a tad wide and wet before a tear escaped. He wiped it away and she made a noise that was a cross between a sniffle and a laugh.

"It was a pretty dress. I'm still pissed no one got to see it."

He smiled and leaned his forehead into hers. "I bet."

"It's been hard stomaching the Christmas season this

year. It's so in your face. Christmas was supposed to be full of love for us, our anniversary, and instead it is full of my heartache. I'm not mad at him anymore, but I have an almost visceral reaction to Christmas now. It brings back all those memories, and my embarrassment, and the pain of being so publicly rejected."

"That's horrible, Sasha. I'm so sorry. This had to be hell for you, being stuck here."

"It wasn't so bad, almost like exposure therapy."

He snorted and kissed her lightly. "I can't imagine leaving someone at the altar. You deserved better than that."

"He said he didn't want to be tied down, wasn't ready, too young. He wasn't right for me—I realize that now. He saved us both a lot of pain down the line."

"Still had to hurt," he said. She shrugged and shot him a sad smile. He trailed a hand from her neck to her shoulder. "How did you cope with the breakup?"

His recent breakup made him feel unimportant and small. He didn't miss his ex, exactly, but he felt dumb for not seeing how unsteady their relationship had been to begin with.

"Well, I coped by fucking one of my bridesmaids—the inimitable Josy. She's part of a monogamous throuple now, so no more playtime for us. But yeah, I fucked a friend, which helped for about an hour or, well, four hours." She smiled but quickly sobered. "Then I didn't get out of bed for three weeks."

He stared at her hard, scared to ask the next question, but it felt inexorable, like the melting of snow and the changing of seasons. "Is he why you don't date? This asshole who broke your heart?"

A little furrow bloomed between her brows as she frowned. "I guess I don't trust in romantic love. For me. I've had no real examples of it in my entire life. My parents sucked and were worse when they were together. My fiancé dumped me and left me to sort out the mess of our cancelled wedding. My sister's going through a messy divorce, and my brother can't find a good man to save his life. Why search for something if it doesn't exist? It's as useful as thinking Santa's actually going to fart out your chimney with a bag of toys."

"But ..." His heart was slamming in his chest, every cell in his body screaming at him to argue.

He wasn't even sure she was wrong. He didn't have many good examples of loving relationships either. His mom and dad had been great together, but his dad had died young. He had friends who were married but just as many who were divorced.

But that didn't mean love wasn't a worthy pursuit or that he didn't want it.

"You're not going to talk me out of it," she said softly. "I'm happy. I have lots of friends and a wonderful, exciting job. Those things fill my life with all the companionship and intimacy and love I need. I get that there are exceptions to the rule, that romance and relationships work for some people. That it doesn't hurt them like it has hurt me. But they're the exceptions."

He nodded and rolled over onto his back. Her words shouldn't have gutted him, but they did.

"I understand why you feel that way. I wish … Well, I like you, but I respect that you don't want that with me."

"It's not only you, Perry. It's everyone. Anyone. You and I—we could be friends. We could definitely fuck again. But not—"

"I get it." He didn't want to hear her reject him again. He took an unsteady breath. "I think … Maybe I crave security and love, especially with my life all over the place. That's what I want."

Two nights with Sasha and his emotions were already getting away from him. There was no way he could do this regularly, not without falling for her.

I don't want to get hurt.

"It's a good thing to want," she said. "It's important to know yourself, to know what works for you and what doesn't."

"But that means that this"— he gestured between them—"doesn't work. Or, that it won't, eventually."

Her jaw clenched, and sadness flooded her eyes for a second before she blinked it away. "Yeah. We had a fun two days, though."

She pulled the sheet up over their heads until they were enclosed in it, intimate and warm. They stared into each other's eyes, memorizing the moment. And each other. He had been in a lot of relationships and had believed himself in love a time or two, but he'd never felt this stripped down. Never wished that morning would never come.

After a few minutes, Sasha yawned, and he pulled her deeper into his arms.

"Is sex always like this for you? Always so ... *close*?" he whispered.

She reached up and cupped his jaw sloppily, her eyelids losing their fight against sleep.

"No. Not like this."

Chapter Eight

_____

The sound of large machinery crunching through the snow woke Sasha up at eight in the morning.

Snowplow.

The snowfall was supposed to have stopped around seven, and Valerie had obviously hired a plow to clear the driveway. The temperature was set to jump above freezing around eight thirty, which should melt the remaining ice on the hill and make it possible for Sasha to leave. There was only a short window, though, as a second round of snow and freezing temperatures was on its way later in the morning.

She watched Perry sleep for several minutes, trying to urge her body out of bed and away from him. Easier said than done. He was warm and cuddly, his handsome face slack with sleep. She wanted to run her fingers through his messy mop of hair and touch the fine bones of his face.

But she did neither of those things.

Sasha didn't want to have an emotional goodbye with Perry. She didn't want to have to see the hurt in his eyes again, because last night it had gutted her.

He didn't stir as she slithered out of bed and silently put her clothes back on. Maybe he was a deep sleeper. What else could she learn about him if she allowed herself to stick around?

As she was about to make the walk-of-shame through the adjoining bathroom, she froze. She wanted to give him something, needed to actually. A gift to remember her by.

She quietly unzipped her red bag and pulled out a box. There was a bright green ribbon on the Christmas tree in the corner of the room, so she filched it and tied a bow around the box. If only she weren't such a Scrooge, she'd be the best Santa in all the land.

As she placed Perry's gift on the bedside table, he reached out and caressed her wrist. She jumped out of her skin and dropped the box onto the hardwood floor.

"*Sweet baby Jesus*, you scared me. You're always making me fumble shit."

"Maybe you're just not very observant." His voice was sleep-roughened and sweet. She smiled at him.

"That's true."

"Is that for me?"

"Yes. I like giving you presents."

He blinked sleepily. "I think you're better at this Christmas thing than you give yourself credit for. You have a generous spirit."

His words hit her in the chest and filled her with a strange longing.

"Go back to sleep. You're not making any sense."

His gaze flitted to the box on the floor, and she had to stifle a giggle. She was ridiculous.

"Is that a prostate massager?" he asked.

"Yes. It's a parting gift."

He laughed. "Well, Happy Holidays to me, I guess."

"You think you'll enjoy it?"

"I do." A blush rose up through his beard. "I've never used one, but fingers are a thing, and I happen to know I like that."

"You're a diamond in the rough, Perry." She leaned in and kissed his mouth tenderly. "You'll be the highlight of my Christmas."

He caught her chin and kissed her harder, but then he let her go.

He let her go.

She shouldn't be sad about that. She wanted him to let her go, but part of her rebelled. Some soft, gooey piece of her heart wanted to spend the perfect Christmas with this man who loved the holiday in a way she'd never understand.

But she wanted safety more. Wanted her heart intact. Wanted to muddle through another holiday season without being heartbroken.

"Bye, Perry."

He shook his head, as if he was trying to wake himself up, but his eyes were already closing.

"Give me a second, and I'll walk you out. To say goodbye."

"No. I want to remember you like this. Warm and rosy and half-asleep. Beautiful. I don't want to drag it out."

His body seemed to slump back on the bed, though he hadn't moved. Maybe it was more of an emotional reaction that she could read in every line of his being.

She patted his leg awkwardly when he didn't say anything. Then she grabbed her bag and moved toward the bathroom door.

"It was nice to meet you," he said.

Such simple words. Meaningless really and cold. Formal. Not full of the emotion she'd seen from him for two days, and it hurt. Hurt worse than she ever could have imagined, which was ironic since heartache was what she'd so wanted to avoid.

"Yep. You too."

She snuck back into her room. She needed to pack her shit and then get the hell out of this Christmas nightmare. Her Lady Robin's bags were easily reassembled. She'd left the Fancy Fleshstroker, the P-Spot Pulse, the Shake and Shimmy Cock Ring, and the Chained Melody Clamps with Perry. She put her red velvet cocktail dress back on, along with the thigh highs for a tad more warmth. It felt like a walk of shame, but she'd walk it with as much confidence and sass as possible.

After making her bed, she took one last look around the room. She wasn't sad to be leaving. She wasn't going to miss this room with its extravagant Christmas decorations, but a strange emptiness was pushing against her ribs. It was a physical weight in her chest, a pain she wasn't sure what to do with.

She deposited the clothes she'd borrowed from Valerie through a laundry chute and dragged her sorry self and her roller bags downstairs.

Valerie was bopping around the kitchen, making donuts in a FryDaddy and putting muffins in the oven.

"Hey, you!" Valerie said when she spotted her, rushing over to give her a hug. "You seem all ready to depart."

"Good morning."

"The ice is already melting off the driveway, and we salted and sanded it, which should help. I think you'd be fine to leave at any time in the next hour or so."

"Have you heard about road conditions back into the city?"

"I saw on the news this morning that the interstate is open." Valerie whisked a cream mixture in a bowl as she talked. Evidently both Winters siblings could multitask. "It will be slow going, especially on the city streets, but the crews have been clearing roads since around three this morning. You should be fine, if you avoid the big hills. And you have my number and Perry's so if you run into any trouble, please call us. Perry's big-ass SUV could make it to you in a jiff."

"Okay. Thanks."

Yeah, there was no way in hell Sasha was going to call Perry after their awkward goodbye.

"You have to at least have an apple cider donut before you leave. Fresh out of the fryer."

"Sure."

Sasha would never turn down a donut. Valerie handed her a piping-hot donut sprinkled in powdered sugar, and Sasha took a big bite.

As Sasha was chewing, Valerie said, "So what's the deal with you and my brother?"

"Hmmm?" Sasha tried to swallow, but the yeasty dough stuck in her throat.

"Just wondering if we'd be seeing you again. You know we have the Winterberry Christmas Couples' Soiree. It's very romantic."

Sasha finally got the lump of donut choked down.

"Oh, well, I don't think so."

"I thought you guys had hit it off."

Sasha stared at her, eyes wide, and all rational thought completely fled her mind. What could she say to that?

I did hit it off with your hot brother, but I'm an emotionally repressed Scrooge with commitment issues. I don't believe in romance or Christmas or any of the tenants of this beautiful business you've created here, the one that's the Winters' legacy.

Valerie laughed. "Holy shit, I put you majorly on the spot. I'm sorry."

"It's fine."

"Damn. On that awkward-as-fuck note, let me walk you out."

Sasha nodded. "Okay."

They trudged out onto the porch together. Water dripped from large icicles hanging from the eaves, and snow blanketed the front lawn. It was still shadowy outside, with the sun low on the horizon, but the snow cover lightened up the dimness. The snow was slushy on the walkways, which was a good sign. It wasn't slick, but it was wet.

The temperature was probably pushing forty, which would make the roads treacherous with black ice in three hours when it re-froze.

Sasha loaded her bags into the backseat of her Bug before turning to Valerie. "I'm happy I met you. All of you."

"Me too. I wish you lived closer so you could be in our book club."

"Will you pass my goodbyes along to Karen, Andie, and Louise?"

"Of course. What about Perry?"

"I said 'bon voyage' to him this morning."

"Okay. That's … something." Valerie frowned, and panic exploded in Sasha's chest. She had to get out of here. This hurt too much.

"Yep." Sasha opened her car door, then turned back to Valerie. "You should ask her out. Louise. She'll say yes."

Valerie smiled and nodded once in acknowledgment. Then Sasha climbed behind the wheel, started the engine, and began the stressful trek up the sloped driveway.

Like two nights ago, her little car struggled at the steepest part in the middle, but this time, it powered through it. It almost felt easy when she crested the top of the hill. She glanced in her rearview mirror to get one last peek at the Winterberry Inn.

It was sparkling with strings of red and green lights

and looked like a Christmas card with pillows of snow on every inch of the yard and roof. But it wasn't the Victorian house itself that pulled her attention.

No, it was Perry standing next to his sister, his arm around her shoulders, watching Sasha leave him.

She pulled onto the main road, going through the motions of driving, as her heartbeat thundered in her ears. Her breath pitched and caught in her throat. She made it to the interstate in a daze before she had to shake herself. It wasn't safe to drive if she couldn't focus.

But that image of Perry, leaning on his sister for comfort, had superimposed itself in her mind's eye. She couldn't *unsee* it. She couldn't believe it would be her last glimpse of him.

Maybe they could continue the friends-with-benefits situation she'd originally suggested.

No.

He'd made it obvious that wouldn't work for him, which she respected. She could compromise, try to open her heart, even though it was the last thing she could imagine doing, especially around Christmas, when she had to be so on guard all the time.

But you've already opened up, said the awful tiny voice in her head. She'd allowed him to burrow beneath her walls, to touch that soft, sensitive part of her heart that she thought was permanently closed for business.

Son of a bitch. Why did he have to be so different? So wonderful?

As she bumped along the snow-packed interstate at

less than thirty miles per hour, her vision fuzzed, and she wiped her cheek.

A tear.

Oh shit. She was crying. Was that why her chest hurt? Why her head was pounding?

An easy exit, with a clear path to a gas station, came into view, so she pulled over and called her sister.

"Rosie, I think I fucked up," she said once the call connected. Her voice was strained, and she hiccupped a sob at the end.

Without missing a beat, her strong, take-charge older sister said, "Emergency brunch. How soon can you get to Jolly's Café? They don't close for anything, and we got less snow on this side of the city."

Jolly's Café was a breakfast and brunch place that was within a mile of all their apartments, because she and her two siblings were obviously co-dependent and lived in each other's pockets. Her brother and sister could walk there.

"It'll be at least an hour and forty-five minutes if I don't go home to change first. Longer if I do."

"Brunch first. Then clean clothes."

"I'm kind of last-night's-mistress this morning." She hadn't even showered off the extraordinary sex and only had a velvet holiday dress to wear.

"Is this walk-of-shame the reason you think you fucked up?"

"Yep."

Rosie paused for a second, probably shocked by that.

Any show of emotion from Sasha over a partner was unusual.

"Then I'd say mimosas are more important than clean undies."

Sasha wasn't wearing undies, but otherwise, she tended to agree.

SASHA FELL UNCEREMONIOUSLY into the seat across from Rosie and Benji. They'd beaten her to Jolly's Café—the roads had been extra slow-going for most of the drive—and claimed their normal booth. Her siblings both sat up straighter, their eyes wide, when she settled in. She took her coat off.

"What the fuck are you wearing?" Benji asked. "It's fab, don't get me wrong. Very Naughty Mrs. Claus, which I love, but wow."

"Shut up."

"And that beard burn. *Damn!*"

"What happened at this bed and breakfast?" Rosie said before Benji could lend more color commentary to the situation. "You'd told me it'd be a boring day of Christmas movies and baked goods."

"And that's what it was." The waitress came by, verified Sasha's ID, then deposited their requisite carafe of mimosas. Once she was gone, Sasha said, "Then I fucked up."

"How?" Rosie asked.

"The Lady Robin's party was hosted by Valerie, the owner of the inn. Her brother, Perry, showed up a day earlier than she expected to try to beat the storm. And he was wonderful." She stopped there, not sure how to explain the hole in her chest or how it pained her to breathe.

She'd told Perry there couldn't ever be anything meaningful between them, just like she'd told countless other people in the last year. Why did it hurt so badly this morning?

"*And?*" Benji asked. "You murdered him? What do you mean you fucked up?"

"She fell for him," Rosie said, a small smile curling the edges of her mouth. Sasha and Rosie looked a lot alike, but Rosie was contained and reserved, whereas Sasha was loud and brash and wild. Right now, Rosie seemed way too proud of herself.

"I don't want a boyfriend," Sasha said stubbornly. "Or a girlfriend. Or a significant other. I want nothing to do with that bullshit."

Benji's big green eyes widened, and he gaped at her. "Holy shit. You fell for some rando at a sex-toy party? You truly are living the best life, sis."

"I didn't fall for some rando."

The waitress came back to take their orders and they each requested the sourdough pancakes, as was emergency brunch tradition, but Benji added the spruce-tip-birch syrup because he was feeling "Christmassy."

Once they were alone again, Rosie reached across the sticky table and grabbed her hand. "P.J. hurt you." Sasha tensed at the mention of her ex, but the ever-solid Rosie didn't pause. "And I understand your reasons for not wanting to settle down right now."

"If by 'not wanting to settle down' you mean she's a free woman with all the sexual agency in the world, then yes," Benji added diplomatically, and Sasha laughed.

God, she loved her siblings.

"Whatever," Rosie said with an eye roll and a bigger smile. "But why do you refuse to consider a deeper relationship? It doesn't have to be a lifetime commitment or even monogamous. We've tried to set you up with people, but it's always like Rejection City up in here. Or No-Strings Poundtown. Help us understand. Is it because you're not ready? Are you still in love with P.J.? Is it because you don't believe in love at all, or you haven't found the right person? Or perhaps you're—"

"Scared," Benji said, suddenly serious, no diplomatic question mark in his voice.

"I'm not scared," Sasha hissed and jerked her hand away.

Their waitress came back with their food, and Rosie ordered a peppermint mocha. Evidently everyone was in the holiday spirit today, except Sasha. She drank down another huge swallow of mimosa, the champagne tickling her nose.

"Then why do you think you fucked up?" Benji asked. "If you don't want to break your relationship embargo for him, then he's obviously not that important."

"Screw you, Benji. He is important," Sasha said, hot and flushed. Benji and Rosie shared a gotcha smile, and

Sasha wanted to face plant into her pancakes. She'd played into their tricky little hands. "I fucked up because I didn't want to say goodbye to him. I let him weasel his way under my defenses, and now I'm screwed."

"Why don't you tell us about him?" Rosie said.

"Fine." Sasha ate a bite angrily, then moaned because the pancakes were so fucking tasty. "He just moved here from Topeka, as in he hasn't even unpacked his vehicle, and is hoping to live with his sister. He used to be an accountant but is enrolled in school starting in the spring for horticulture and landscape architecture. He's sweet, expressive, willing to experiment. Great in bed. He loves romance novels and Christmas. I don't know. I liked him." She lifted her shoulders, despair souring the food in her stomach.

"So he's perfect," Benji said, pretending to swoon into Rosie, the back of his hand on his forehead.

"Except for the whole homeless, jobless thing," Rosie added, playfully shoving Benji away.

"He has a plan, though and doesn't seem to be a flake," Sasha said.

Rosie tapped a pink fingernail against her bottom lip. "You keep defending him. You like him, Sasha. What's holding you back?"

"*She scared*," Benji whispered, pretending Sasha couldn't hear him.

"Yes, fine. Okay. I'm scared. Wouldn't you be? The last time I fell for a Christmas-loving, softhearted asshole, he literally *left me at the altar*. P.J. was a good guy too. He was sweet and open and we matched. I thought we fit. I can't trust … myself. I can't trust myself."

The aisle at their wedding flashed in her eyes, unwanted and painful. It had been lined with candles and Douglas fir garland. After Rosie had informed the guests that the wedding was off, Sasha had sat down at the end of that beautiful, festive aisle and bawled her eyes out. Tears pricked her eyes at the memory, the embarrassment rushing up on her like heartburn.

She took a shuddering breath. "The anniversary of my jilting is days away. It's hard to imagine allowing myself to be open ever again. Also, look around. Benji, how many men have cheated on or ghosted you?" She ignored his indignant disagreement. "And Rosie, you're currently waist deep in divorce lawyers! You can't even be in the same room with he-who-shall-not-be-named. Our parents hated each other. And—"

"Stop." Sasha reeled back at Rosie's quiet voice. It was her teacher voice, and it worked wonders on tiny children, as well as grown-ass adults. "I am not you. Benji isn't you. Our parents are immaterial. They don't count. The jerks Benji and I have dated *or married* are not … what's his name again? Percy?"

"Perry," Sasha said, her voice small.

"Perry. That's a sweet name. He sounds nice. If you don't believe in relationships because they're not right for you or you know they won't ever fulfill you, then fine. If you're not ready, I understand that, and we'll support you. But don't you dare blame not wanting a relationship on me and Benji."

Sasha stared at her sister for a long moment, her heart lumped in her throat. Benji's eyes were wide.

Then the floodgates opened. No rhyme or reason for it. Maybe it was her sister's strong, soft voice—she hated feeling like she'd gotten in trouble. Maybe it was the lack of sleep. Or maybe it was that she was facing down her belief system, the core of herself, that she'd been holding onto so tightly, and it was crumbling.

Once the tears hit her cheeks, Rosie yelped in surprise and knocked over her empty mimosa glass while reaching for her.

"*Oh shit*, Sasha. I'm so sorry!" Rosie said.

Both Benji and Rosie rushed to Sasha's side of the booth and enveloped her in their arms. Which made her cry harder.

"I'm sorry. Don't be nice to me. It's making it worse," she said with a sniffle, when Benji kissed her temple.

He laughed, and Rosie rubbed her back vigorously. "It's okay. You're allowed to cry."

"I hate Christmas," she said with a wet laugh. "Saying goodbye to him today sucked. I gave him a prostate massager as a gift." She hiccupped a little. "And he was so funny and charming about it, and I didn't want to leave. I wanted to kiss him again and see him again. But he doesn't want to be friends-with-benefits. He's a romantic."

Benji cupped her cheeks between his hands. "You are my hero. A prostate massager to your one-night stand? God, I wish I was as ballsy as you."

"Two-night stand," Sasha corrected him.

Rosie brought them back to the issue at hand. "Sasha, you have to tell him how you feel."

"I don't know."

Wouldn't taking that jump be better than never seeing him again, never experiencing his rough, greedy kisses? She couldn't imagine never handing him another sex toy, never seeing him laugh or blush. She wanted to see the things he created out of seeds and wood and mulch, wanted to experience the gardens he built when they were in bloom and beautiful.

She closed her eyes, a fissure shooting through her resolve like someone had taken a nutcracker to her heart.

Her life yawned out in front of her, and it suddenly seemed barren. Not because she'd be unhappy living it the way she had for so long. Romance and love weren't required to feel complete or content. She hadn't been lying when she'd said she had all the love, connection, and intimacy she needed, that her life was full and good.

But her life was missing Perry Winters.

It was a puzzle piece clicking into place. She didn't need him to be happy. But she *wanted* him. She wasn't sure she could let him in completely. It might take work. It might hurt at moments and end in heartache. But maybe he was worth it.

Not maybe.

He *was* worth it.

She hadn't thought she'd ever be willing to risk her heart again.

But Perry was … special.

"I think he's worth it." She scrubbed a stray tear off her cheek. "Worth the possibility of pain."

"Christmas is about possibility, Sasha," Benji said with a big grin. "You got screwed in the Christmas karma department last year. The world owes you a big strapping Christmas hero. He is strapping, right?"

Perry had said he loved Christmas because of the possibility in the air, the potential. Maybe he'd been on to something.

"He's strapping."

"And does he want you?" Rosie asked, always the logical one.

"He did. But I kind of rejected him."

There was no *kind of* about it. She'd rejected him.

"We need a scheme," Benji said with a triumphant cackle. He'd had the most mimosas that morning. "A Christmas scheme. You're the Grinch, and he's the schoolgirl that cured the black hole where your heart used to be."

"He's Cindy Lou Who," Rosie whispered, excitement and awe in her voice. Evidently, even Sasha's rational, reasonable sister could be moved by the spirit of the season.

"A Christmas scheme," Sasha repeated, her mind reeling with all the things Perry had said he loved about Christmas—the possibility in the air, the romance, the excitement. "I think I know exactly who could help."

Chapter Nine

*V*alerie woke Perry up from his doze on the couch with a mug of eggnog.

"Hey, Val."

"Hey, sleepyhead."

"Sorry I passed out on you."

"It's okay. You needed the shut-eye. You've got dark circles. Looks like you've been punched."

He felt like it too.

He hadn't slept much since the snow-pocalypse had passed and everyone had gone back to their regularly scheduled lives. Including Sasha.

He was moping, basically. Sad that he'd felt a connection that evidently wasn't there. Mad at himself for wanting to push when she wasn't interested.

He was also exhausted from a busy morning setting up for the Soiree. The enormous formal dining room had been converted into a romantic dance floor, with a small portable stage at one end for a band. There were candles all over the main floor of the inn, which would lend the night an intimate ambiance. Mistletoe had been hung from every doorway. Hors d'oeuvres would be circulated and wine would flow. The backyard path to the gazebo had been cleared and heaters, along with candles and boxwood wreathes, adorned the cozy white structure.

It had been a busy few days. He'd helped with the planning and setup for the party, as well as moved into the carriage house with Valerie. He hadn't wanted to take up a room that she could be selling.

When he and Valerie hadn't been elbow deep in party planning, they'd gorged on cheesy Christmas movies. He wanted to remember why he loved this season, why it filled him with awe and excitement. But if watching holiday movies had taught him anything, it was that love was in the air at Christmas. Too bad it had only infected one party.

He took a long gulp of his eggnog and only then did he notice Valerie's clothes.

"Oh shit, what time is it?"

She was already in her party dress, a tight black thing with a wine-red belted bow. He wasn't into fashion, but the dress was perfect on her. Her cheeks were rosy, her eyes done up, her long curly hair pulled into a sophisticated topknot.

"It's five. You need to get your fancy duds on before the guests arrive."

She pinched him above his knee, catching the ticklish nerves there, causing him to flinch and slop eggnog onto his wrist.

Older sisters could be the worst.

He wasn't really attending the party, but he planned to help Valerie coordinate the event and step in as wait-staff if need be.

He pulled himself off Valerie's couch and rubbed a hand down his face. The thought of being around a house full of romance made his stomach curdle. Normally, he'd be so excited to be around happy couples who were in love.

Not today. Not on the tail end of a rejection that had gutted him more than his last real breakup.

"I invited Louise tonight," Valerie said right as Perry made it to the threshold of the living room. He pivoted back around slowly.

"Did you now? That's exciting." He tried to keep his tone as casual as possible. Valerie had been talking herself out of making a move on Louise for years.

"Yeah. We'll see. I'll be busy, but I wanted her here."

"I'm proud of you, Val."

"Sasha gave me that final push to take the plunge."

He gaped at her. "What do you mean?" Hearing Sasha's name sent a shaft of longing through him.

Valerie shrugged and smiled sheepishly. "Sasha told me to ask Louise out, to take the chance. It helped to hear it from an outside observer. I wasn't sure Louise was actually interested."

"I've been telling you forever that she is." A mulish frown pulled at his lips.

"Better not pout, Perry. Santa doesn't like it. You're my brother. You're not objective."

"I can't believe Sasha gave you dating advice," he grumbled. "She's anti-relationship."

"I know, bub."

"She'll push you to ask someone out, but she won't even consider going on a date with me."

"I'm sorry."

"Why am I mad about this? She's allowed to feel the way she feels. I understand her position. But I thought she didn't have a romantic bone in her body, and here she is convincing you to ask out the woman you've been crushing on for years. That shouldn't make me feel so … confused, should it?"

"It's okay to be confused." There was an odd glint in Valerie's eye, like she found Perry hilarious.

He growled. "Never mind. I'm putting on my accounting slacks."

Valerie laughed at that. "Wear your suspenders. You'll look hipster hot."

"No reason for me to look hot," he said under his breath as he left the room. "The woman I want won't be here."

THE TURNOUT for the Soiree was rocking. Perry had wondered if the crowd would be smaller than usual, since so many people had lost shopping days during the snow-pocalypse. He'd worried that people would opt for a night at the mall rather than a romantic evening at the local inn.

But couples littered the property like pairs of turtledoves or, in some cases, triads of French hens. He offered a tray of wine and chocolate to two men that were cuddled up in the hearth room as the retro band Valerie hired, Cherry and the Pits, struck up a rendition of "Have Yourself a Merry Little Christmas."

Both men declined the wine, though one of them took a chocolate-covered strawberry, as they stood up to dance right there in the hearth room. That had been one of the most fascinating parts of this party to Perry when he was a child and spying on the party guests. People slow-danced anywhere and everywhere on the grounds, as if they were so moved by the romance, by the magic of Christmas, by each other, that they just had to hold each other and sway *right then.*

A vision of dancing with Sasha in the attic to Eartha Kitt, *of undressing with Sasha to Eartha Kitt,* hit Perry so suddenly it was like a physical punch. He smiled at the men, then moved back into the kitchen where he was essentially alone.

He pressed his palms into the cold granite countertop and hung his head.

Shake it off. Let it go.

She wasn't yours to keep.

The smoky voice of the lead singer of Cherry and the Pits transitioned between songs with a bit of mellow banter. The sound soothed Perry.

He moved back toward the formal dining room. The

flicker of the candlelight chased him through the house. The other lights in the house were dimmed except for the strings on the Christmas trees and garland. It lent the house a romantic air.

He caught sight of his sister talking with a glowing Louise near one of the large windows. Their heads were close together, secret smiles shared between them.

Cherry and the Pits began a slow, melancholy version of his favorite Christmas song—"I'll Be Home For Christmas." The lead singer started the song acapella, her sweet voice floating through the house. Couples danced all around Perry, so he squeezed into a corner of the room and closed his eyes. Once the piano joined the singer's voice, Perry's breath caught. It was beautiful.

Moving, slow, and almost sad.

She stopped singing, but the piano accompaniment continued. And it was perfect.

Perry kept his eyes shut and let the music wash over him.

"Hi, everyone," a voice filtered through the mic, the pianist still playing in the background.

Perry jerked off the wall and nearly knocked over a wrought-iron candelabra. His heart lurched into his throat.

Sasha.

This felt like a trick or a bad twist of fate. Was he being Christmas Punk'd?

Didn't matter. He ate Sasha up with his eyes. She was wearing a vintage-y dark green satin dress with a full, knee-length skirt. Her hair was styled up into a pompadour with winterberries clipped behind her ear. She was feminine, and edgy, and retro all at once, and his heart broke at how much seeing her soothed his soul.

"I'm Sasha. I pulled a big favor in order to be standing up here, so thank you for indulging me. I should have worn a Scrooge costume, but Dame Winterberry herself—Ms. Valerie—vetoed that. See, I hate Christmas."

Movement on the edge of his vision pulled his attention away. It was Valerie and Louise scooting closer to him through the crowd. The music was playing in the background, soft and expressive, almost a bluesy version of the song.

"What's happening?" he whispered to his sister. She shushed him with a grin and a wink.

"Let me put it this way," Sasha continued. "I *hated* Christmas until I met a wonderful man who is the epitome of the holiday season. He's everything that's special about it. He's cheerful, jolly, and sweet as spiced eggnog. He makes me want to ride a sleigh, and ice skate, and window shop while holding hands in the snow. All these clichés that seemed so silly before, now seem essential, if only I get to do them with him. He sees the potential of the season, he believes in love and romance, and good Lord, his lips deserve a constant sprig of mistletoe, let me tell you."

Perry finally allowed himself to move from his perch in the corner. Everyone parted for him to walk to the front, watching him curiously. He couldn't take his eyes off her.

She smiled at him. "But I screwed it up because when he asked me for a date, when he told me he wanted to make this Christmas my best Christmas, I told him *no*."

Joy welled up inside him.

This was a grand gesture. Sasha was grand gesturing for him.

"Perry, I regret telling you *no*. I was scared. I'd like that date, please. I have it all planned out. First things first, we'll go to this crazy romantic party thrown at this ridiculously cozy B and B because I can't imagine enjoying this with anyone, except you. With you, it'll be spectacular. With you, I think anything would be spectacular."

The crowd chuckled appreciatively at her joke. He was at the front of the crowd now. She stepped away from the microphone, and he gently lifted her down from the stage. He vaguely heard cheers as he caught her beautiful face in his hands and kissed her like it was raining mistletoe.

"Whew, that could have gone horribly wrong," the lead singer said as she reached the mic again. Then she started another verse of "I'll Be Home For Christmas."

"Will you dance with me?" Sasha asked, her cheeks pink and her hands shaking.

He couldn't speak. Couldn't believe she was here for him. He pulled her close and held her like he couldn't, wouldn't ever let her go.

She rested her temple against his cheek, and they swayed to the sweet music, caught up in their own world, their own song.

Once the song was over, Perry kissed her ear. "I want to show you something."

"Is it dirty? Because I'm in for dirty."

Laughing, he tugged her deeper into his arms. "No. We're not hiding behind that. I've always dreamed of bringing a woman to the Soiree. I don't want this to end yet."

She ducked her head and snaked her hands up his back.

"I don't want it to end either. You look handsome, by the way. I love the suspenders and bowtie. And see, we match."

She held up her sleeve of satin. The deep shiny green matched the darkest forest on his plaid bowtie.

Pressing his forehead to hers, he said, "We match. We fit. Follow me. I'm going to show you the prettiest place on the property tonight."

She tipped her head back and met his eyes. A slice of fear flickered through her gaze.

"Don't be scared," he said.

She smiled. "Lead the way."

Perry held tight to Sasha's hand as he led her through the house. Candlelight made her skin glow.

"We need to grab our coats."

They made their way to the coat check to retrieve hers. It was that same green trench. The color on her reminded him of Santa's elves, especially with her pixie-ish face. She was gorgeous—vibrant and fun and sunny. He grabbed his coat and scarf from the coat closet by the front door.

His heart felt too big for his chest, and he couldn't stop kissing her. In fact, they'd had to stop every twenty feet so he could press his joy into her lips again and again. Eventually, they made it to the back door. He opened it and escorted her out into the cold.

There was still snow on the ground but not as much as the days before. The temperature was below freezing tonight, but the sky was clear and the moon bright. Christmas lights lined the walkway to the gazebo. An older couple was snuggling on the swing on the back porch, but other than them, they were alone out here.

They reached the gazebo, which was alight with warm lanterns and candles. Several heaters kept the small circular space toasty, despite the biting cold outside. A speaker piped in the music from Cherry and the Pits.

Sasha turned in a circle, her skirt swirling around her legs, and his pulse hitched, his heart soaring. She stopped with her back to him, gazing toward a huge white pine tree dripping in snow and colorful Christmas lights.

"It's beautiful," she breathed. "I can admit that now, right? That you guys here at Winterberry know how to make Christmas beautiful."

He needed to see her here among the candles—her cheeks and nose rosy from the cold, lights reflecting in her big blue eyes, so he turned her slowly back toward him. He tipped her chin up, and she parted her kissable lips.

"*You're* beautiful."

The corners of her lips quirked. "What if all this between us is Christmas fever? What if it wears off?"

"It won't," he said. "For me, it won't."

"You're so sure after two nights together?"

"Aren't you? Because you just stood up on a stage in front of a large crowd and admitted your undying devotion," he teased.

She playfully pushed him away, then reeled him back in and kissed him soundly on the lips. "I'm sure. More than I've been in a long time. It's not me I'm worried about."

He cupped her cheeks and thumbed her berry-red bottom lip. He had gloves in his coat pocket but preferred the warmth of her skin to the scratchy wool. "You inspire me. You brighten up every room you're in. You're hilarious and brash and beautiful. I want to spend as much time in your orbit as possible. My life is in shambles, and I know it'll take time to earn your trust. And I also know that nothing is guaranteed. But, Sasha, I've never been so positive that someone is special and that what we feel for each other is special. I knew it the moment you dropped the Pulse 2 on my sister's hardwood floor."

She laughed, her eyes twinkling and her breath frosting in the cold air. "I'm really good at first impressions."

He pressed their foreheads together. "You're so brave. Coming here, standing on that stage."

"Your sister told me that was your favorite Christmas song. Which is silly. The best Christmas song is obviously 'Good King Wenceslas.'"

He laughed. He should have realized Valerie had a hand in this. "Obviously. It wouldn't have been as romantic, though."

"And you're Mr. Romance. I had a lot to live up to."

He threaded his fingers into her hair. It was slightly crunchy with hair product, and he enjoyed the texture against his palms. "You don't have to live up to anything. You need to be yourself. You're pretty miraculous just as you are."

"Even as a Scrooge?"

She slipped her hands to his stomach and gripped his sides.

He melted in her hold. "Especially as a Scrooge. Keeps me on my mistletoes."

A crack of a laugh burst from her. "That was horrible."

"You liked it."

"I did." She crowded her body into his, and he realized they were swaying to the beat.

"Sasha, it feels like I'm finally right where I'm meant to be."

"I think you are." She tilted her head slightly to kiss his cheek, then the hinge of his jaw. He gripped her hips and drew her closer. She whispered in his ear. "So once this merry shindig is over, I think we should head back to my place. Maybe we can start making our own Christmas traditions. You know, watch a couple Christmas horror movies, bake a fruitcake, role play Santa and his naughty elf."

Perry grinned, happiness making him reckless. He lifted her and tossed her over his shoulder. Her peals of laughter made him walk faster. "Let's go, naughty elf. Time to leave," he said.

"Who says I'm the elf? I'm the one with all the toys!"

Perry stopped in his tracks and set her back on her feet on the top step of the gazebo. "That is so true." Then he kissed her, long and lingering, until they were both grinning and alight with joy.

Epilogue

*S*asha handed Perry his fuzzy red Christmas stocking before flopping over in bed to kiss his hipbone. She knew, after a year together, that it would make him shudder. And it did. His head also hitched back, his fingers finding a home in her short hair. Dim, wintery morning light filtered in through Perry's apartment window, illuminating his bare skin. The window was frosted from the cold air, but this year they weren't lucky enough to have a white Christmas.

After a few seconds, he said, "Let me grab your stocking. It's under my bed."

She gladly rolled off his legs because she was thrilled about this new tradition. She hadn't been excited about getting presents since she was a kid, but the thought of what Perry might have stuffed her stocking with was enough to make her bubbly with eagerness.

Really, this whole holiday season had proven her to be the epitome of eagerness, from choosing trees at a

Christmas tree farm to ice skating in the city to a date at the symphony to hear the Gay Men's Chorus Christmas Concert. Seeing Perry's pure love and celebration of the season had made her feel like a child discovering Santa's workshop, all fervor and hope and happiness.

And now, here they were on Christmas morning, and Sasha hadn't once felt the suffocating pressure of the holidays, not like in the past. Plus, this year, there were stockings!

Perry leaned over the side of his queen-sized bed, giving her a smoking view of his back and ass, which she grabbed, of course, before he reappeared with a green Christmas stocking filled to the brim with presents. She sat cross-legged on the bed, her flannel nightie riding up around her thighs, and smiled at her beautiful boyfriend.

He grinned lazily back.

"God, Christmas is the best," he said.

"Oh yeah? Why?"

"Well, for one, you bought me my favorite lube." He pulled the bottle out of the top of his stocking. "Two, I have three whole days off before I'm due back at the nursery."

Sasha smiled and rubbed his leg happily. Perry had gotten a part-time job at Boon's Nursery and Tree Farm shortly after the New Year. He'd been supplementing that income with seasonal accounting work for a personal tax company in addition to attending classes, which he loved. Last week, he and Sasha had started on a business plan for his own company. That was still years away but filled her with excitement and pride for his dreams. She couldn't wait to see them come to fruition.

"And three, I'm spending it with my favorite person in the world." He reached out and cupped Sasha's cheek. She kissed the base of his thumb, then the center of his palm.

It was hard for her some days. Hard to trust that this wasn't false or too good to be true. But Perry trusted her to get over her insecurities, and he believed in the power of them together. She never doubted that she'd made the right decision by jumping onto that stage last year and putting her heart on the line.

"Dump that baby out." She waved at his stocking. "We have four hours before we're due to meet the whole fam at the inn for Christmas dinner, and I expect to use every second of it."

Their little clans had meshed into one crazy, happy family. Sasha's siblings were thick as thieves with Valerie and Louise—they all enjoyed torturing and teasing Perry and Sasha together. And Perry's mom, Rhoda, and her hot young boyfriend, Brand, had made the trip from Hawaii to spend Christmas here. Sasha loved Perry's mom. She had the outgoing irreverence of Valerie with the sweetness and compassion of Perry.

However, their family felt miles away as they both emptied their stockings, making Perry's bed a filthy winter wonderland. There were plugs and clamps and vibrators and cock rings and lingerie.

Once they'd opened every last present, Sasha closed

her eyes and hummed deep in her throat. "God, I adore our relationship."

Perry grabbed a Santa hat from the pile of toys. It had the words *I Love Snowballs* embroidered on the white trim and had made Sasha giggle so hard when she'd spotted it online that she'd been forced to impulse buy.

He slapped it on his head and said, "Your pick, sweetheart."

She grinned, excited that he was letting her choose. Every once in a while, Perry took over in bed, normally when he'd been teased to within an inch of his life, but usually he was happy to let Sasha have her wicked way.

She quickly grabbed up everything she wanted to keep on the bed with them—silky bondage straps, lube, and a fancy new prostate toy—and pushed the rest unceremoniously off the bed.

Perry helped her wash the new toys off quickly with toy-disinfecting wipes. Then he yanked her flannel nightie off and flung it across the room as if it had offended him. She immediately shivered against the chill in the room, her nipples tightening and goosebumps blooming across her skin. Perry tumbled her onto her back and blanketed her with his body heat.

"I love you," he whispered in her ear after leaving a trail of kisses up her neck. "I love you so much."

She threaded her fingers into his curly hair, trembling as his beard scratched against her skin. "I love you too, Perry."

A weight always lifted off her shoulders when she

admitted that, when she said it out loud, making her feel light and airy and free.

"What do you want to do? Who gets the silk?" he asked, smiling against her throat. They mixed it up often enough that it was a necessary question.

"Me."

"Okay. I have something I'd like for you to put on first. But only if you want it. You can say no."

That piqued her curiosity. "Sure. What is it?"

He reached for the bedside table. His hands were shaking.

"Babe, what's wrong?" she asked.

"Nothing. Just nervous." He straightened up, and only then did she see the tiny red velvet box in his hand.

Surprise, quickly followed by joy, suffused her and she said the first thing that popped into her brain. "Oh my God, I'm naked."

He barked out a laugh. "Should I wait until you're not?"

"No, I think this is pretty standard for us."

They were both laughing when he kissed her and tears filled her eyes when he whispered, "You're my true love, and you give me so much—happiness, joy, love, laughter, understanding, acceptance—and frankly, those things top milking maids and jumping lords and loud birds any day. I'll cherish you forever. I'll love you forever. I'll spend the rest of my life chasing your smile. I'll happily do so in whatever role you'd prefer. As your boyfriend. As your boy toy." She laughed again, the tears spilling down her cheeks. "As your husband. I'd really love to be your husband."

"Okay," she managed to choke out.

"Sasha, is that a *yes*?" His eyes were wide, like he couldn't believe it.

"You haven't actually asked me anything. For all I know that box could be filled with tiny sex toys."

He grinned, his cheeks flushed and eyes bright, and popped the box open to reveal a simple gold ring with a modest emerald stone. "Will you marry me?"

"Fuck yes, I will!"

He whooped in happiness and triumph, his hands thrown into the air, before she yanked him down onto the bed to celebrate.

Over an hour later, after Sasha had worked Perry's new prostate massager into him, which always made him shaky and weak and fucking gorgeous, and he'd tied her ankles to the footboard of his bed, she fisted his curly hair as he ate her out.

The glint of her engagement ring threw her, upped the desire zipping through her nerves as his tongue circled her clit. Perry had written over every bad Christmas memory and every horrible experience she'd had with his nimble tongue and his laugh and the lovelight in his eyes. And he'd continue to do so for the rest of their lives. She twisted against the bonds, loving the resistance of the soft silk on her legs.

He groaned, a rough hungry sound, and yanked her back into place. She shattered against his mouth, sobbing out her pleasure and her love for him, until it was too much and she had to tug his mouth from her swollen, pulsing center. He sat up onto his knees and stared at her. His beard was wet from her and, geez, that was probably her favorite sight in the entire world. She couldn't believe she'd get to see it forever.

She fumbled the remote in her hand, but once she managed to get her thumb on the trigger button, she met his eyes.

"Oh fuck, oh fuck," he chanted, before she'd even done anything.

Then she pressed the button, which turned on the vibration on the P-Spot 3. His head hitched back as if he'd been punched, which, in a way, he had. The muscles in his chest and abdomen stood out in stark relief, veins bulging on his arms, his tattoos and body hair gleaming with sweat. He almost reached for his cock, which was hard and thick and pearling with pre-come at the tip, his hand close to connecting with the rosy head before he snatched his palm away.

He put the Santa hat back on—it had fallen off when he'd been servicing her so thoroughly. Her mind was a bit blurry from her orgasm, but she knew she needed him inside right that instant.

"In. Me. Now," she said, her voice raspy and tight. She ripped open a condom and practically threw it at him. He rolled it down his length with shaking, careful hands, his eyes wild at that barest touch against his cock.

"I'm not going to last inside you for longer than a second, sweetheart. I'm barely hanging on." Nevertheless, he knee-walked toward her. She sat up and licked his chin, her arousal a tart burst on her tongue.

"Tell me how it feels," she said.

"Like my body's on fire. Full. Overwhelmed. Everything is tight and swollen and ..." He gulped and she collapsed back onto the bed. He teased the head of his cock across her clit, then down between the lips of her pussy. "Needy. I feel so needy."

His words sparked over her skin, and excitement made her body flush hot. She loved when he got like this. Uncontrollable. Greedy.

Needy.

Lord, she loved him needy.

He licked his thumb, getting it messy with spit before rubbing it over her clit, hitting her with precisely the right amount of movement and pressure. She whined, still sensitive from her orgasm. She needed something large and hard to counteract that overstimulation.

Perry gave her exactly what she desired. He slid into her slowly, with so much power and strength, it turned her to jelly.

Her eyelids dropped to slits, and she stared up through her lashes at the man she loved more than life itself, as he came immediately, just like he'd warned.

A funny little laugh burst from his throat as his orgasm shook through him, his eyes rolling back and bliss slackening his mouth. Because she was naughty, she used the remote to increase the vibration inside him before his climax could peter off.

He shouted, his voice high and feral, before bucking

into her hard, again and again, chasing every last dredge of pleasure he could. He fell onto one elbow above her, his other hand working magic against her clit, and bit her nipple hard, smothering his own cries for mercy.

She saw stars, her orgasm long and rolling. When she finally opened her eyes, she realized Perry had wrestled the remote from her fingers to turn off the prostate massager. He was resting his forehead against her clavicle, pressing open-mouthed kisses to her flushed chest and collarbones.

"This was the best Christmas ever," she said into the sudden silence.

He lifted his head, bringing her left hand to his lips and kissing her fingers, one of them adorned with a ring. Then with a few quick tugs, he untied the binds around her ankles.

"Next year will be better," he said. "And every year after that. Maybe not as *intense* as this year." He sent her a tiny, ornery smile and she laughed. "Or as life-changing." He ran a thumb over the engagement ring. "Every day we spend together is only going to make me love you more fiercely, more completely. Each year will be a gift, the best Christmas gift I could ever ask for, because I'll get to spend it with you."

Emotion stuck in her throat, and she tried to cough it away. "So can I preemptively veto a Christmas wedding?"

He touched her chin, a small smile on his lips. "Definitely. We should have one of those hipster-chic weddings on a ho-hum Saturday in June like every other millennial in the Midwest."

"It could be in a barn!"

He nodded solemnly. "It'd have to be. Them's the rules."

"As long as your sister makes those fig and goat cheese tarts, I'm there. In fact, I think I'd marry you for those tarts alone." She wrapped her arms around his neck. "I know exactly the wedding I want."

"Oh you do? And what is that?"

"I want to get married in the butterfly garden at the inn with only our family there. I want to be surrounded by flowers you planted in a garden you created and love."

He nudged their noses together, his lips almost trembling. "I adore that idea."

"No poinsettias."

"Agreed, that'd make no sense in the summer."

"Or evergreen garland." She said this like a threat, like he was arguing with her, even though he wasn't.

"I can live with that."

"No pinecones, no matter how pretty you paint them, either."

"Goodness, Sasha, I'm agreeing with you."

She laughed, full of joy. "I'll allow one piece of Christmas only. Maybe clip some into my hair or put some in my bouquet."

"Oh yeah? And what's that?"

She kissed him softly. "Winterberries."

More SO OVER THE HOLIDAYS!

Ready for more of the Holiday siblings?

Candy Hearts and *Bottle Rocket* will be coming your way in 2020!

To keep updated on the SO OVER THE HOLIDAYS series, join my newsletter or Facebook Reader Group.

LIFE OF BLISS - A Short Excerpt

Read on for a small taste of *Life of Bliss*, a fake boyfriends to accidental drunk wedding romance!

Pretending to be boyfriends is easy. Being accidental husbands is not.

Victor woke up with a start, and immediately regretted it. His pulse was throbbing in his temples, and his ears were ringing. He groaned and rubbed his eyes, which was when he realized Todd's tie was looped loosely around his wrist.

"What the hell?" he murmured and yanked it off. Todd rolled over and let out a rumbling sigh in his sleep.

What time is it? Victor reached for his phone, which was plugged in but on the floor for some reason. *Ten fifteen.*

Is that a.m. or p.m.? He had no idea. Except it was dark. So nighttime.

He couldn't remember ever waking up so disoriented.

They must have fallen asleep during the early evening—he couldn't remember eating dinner either.

He placed his phone back on the bedside table.

Which was when he noticed it.

Victor sat up so fast that dizziness almost took him back down. And it only got worse. He stared at his left hand and started trembling.

It was all rushing back now. *Oh, fuck.* He remembered it all. Probably because he hadn't actually been *that* drunk. Definitely not blackout drunk, which would have been the only excuse for *this*.

He grabbed his phone again and pulled up his photos app. *Yep*, it was all there. Proof of everything. From a selfie with the Uber driver who'd taken them to the County Clerk's Office and pictures of their ceremony at some hokey tourist trap to a video of them fucking.

An hour and a half later, Todd woke up, and by that point, Victor had already analyzed every photo—and one raunchy video—that they'd taken that day in painstaking detail, and then cried for thirty minutes in the bathroom. He felt like he deserved a bit of a self-pitying cry. Frankly, he'd gotten exactly what he'd wanted, just not the way he wanted it, and it was about to blow up in his face. Spectacularly.

"Come back to bed," Todd said, his voice sweet. Victor might never hear that tone again. Not once Todd remembered.

Oh, fuck. What if he doesn't remember?

Victor crawled into bed and straddled Todd's lap. He tapped Todd's cheek. "Wake up."

Todd laughed. "I'm awake. Geez." He touched Victor's throat, running his fingers down and along his collarbones, which about split Victor apart in agony. This was all over, and that hurt more than he could handle right now.

"How much do you remember about earlier today?"

"Huh? Everything. Why?" Todd's forehead wrinkled up adorably, and Victor started shaking again. This was so bad.

Then Todd sat up so fast they banged heads, which was worse than the dizziness that had hit Victor when he'd remembered. Todd stared at him, his eyes wild, like his world had just ended. He held up his left hand and saw the yellow silicone ring, and his jaw dropped. He didn't say anything, though, and that was almost scarier than the cursing and recriminations Victor had expected.

"Todd," he said, his voice timid. It made him feel sick, this fear.

"We fucked up," Todd finally said.

That sentence made Victor laugh for some reason. Maybe the matter-of-factness of it. Maybe the absurdity of this situation. Maybe his own panic.

"We fucked up," Victor repeated, pressing the words into Todd's shoulder. Todd's arms circled his waist, and that one little touch sent a wave of relief through him. "How much do you remember?"

"Everything. Oh my God, Vic. What were we thinking?"

Victor shook his head. He had no idea. He kept trying to get back to that moment, the one when it had stopped being a tease and had turned into something so necessary they couldn't resist. But even though he could remember every move they'd made, he couldn't seem to recapture that feeling.

Maybe if he could, he'd know what to do now.

"We made a sex tape," he said.

Todd gently lifted Victor's head from his shoulder and stared at him very seriously. "We need to delete that from the Cloud." Laughter tinged the edges of his voice.

"I already did. It's still on my phone though. Do you want to see?"

"Definitely, but not right now."

Victor nodded. "You tied me to the bed, and I called you '*husband*.'"

It was a pretty hot video. If Victor weren't freaking out so much, he'd probably be impressed. But hearing himself call Todd his husband at the end of it had been too much.

Todd dropped his face into his hands, which forced Victor to back up. It cut him out of this moment, cut him off completely. He climbed off Todd's lap.

"I think I'm having a panic attack. I've never had one, though," Todd whispered, his breath suddenly coming fast.

That was a depressing thought. Being married to Victor was so awful that Todd was having his first-ever panic attack. *Great.*

Victor shook his head, trying to clear it. This wasn't about him, and he needed to get over himself. He grabbed Todd's hands, which were clenched.

"You're hyperventilating, babe. Breathe with me. Nice and slow." Todd nodded and complied, his breath stuttering and shallow. Victor rubbed Todd's palms. "It's going to be okay. Don't think about anything but breathing. I'll make it okay. I promise."

He loved Todd enough to figure it out. And that was also a depressing thought. He loved Todd. Like full-blown, glitter-in-his-brain, hearts-in-his-eyes, bleed-for-him love.

It sucked.

"What are we going to do?" Todd asked, choking on the words. "We got married at a place called Madam Kitty's Old Timey Photos and Brothel! I'm pretty sure I was wearing a cowboy hat."

"You were, but don't think about that. Breathe."

Eventually, Todd's shoulders unhitched from his ears, and the wrinkles in his forehead smoothed out. Some color returned to his face.

"What are we going to do?" he asked again.

"What do you want to do?"

"I have no idea." Todd's voice held so much confused anguish that it broke Victor's heart. "I can't handle this right now. Please, just—"

Victor interrupted Todd, his blood rushing in his ears. "It's okay, babe. You're going to be okay. I'll fix this." He pressed his hand to Todd's chest. His throat hurt from crying, and he felt like his heart was about to crash into the sea. "We can sleep on it tonight and then figure out annulment, if that's what you want. Or file for divorce tomorrow . . ." He sucked in a breath, and laid it all on the line. "Or stay married. I think I'd make a pretty good husband, if you wanted me."

Buy *Life of Bliss* today!

Life of Bliss
© 2018 Erin McLellan

Farm College Series

Controlled Burn

Clean Break

Love Life Series

Life on Pause

Life of Bliss

Storm Chasers Series

Natural Disaster

Acknowledgments

Huge thanks to Edie Danford for her insightful editing, Susie Selva for her wonderful proofreading, Cate Ashwood for creating such a rocking cover, Judith at A Novel Take PR for excellent promo, my beta readers—Allison, Lisa, and Karen—for championing this book early on, and Layla for the extra special help with the dreaded blurb.

Extra hugs to my husband and my family.

Lastly, I couldn't do this job without the readers who keep picking up my books. I'm so thankful for all of you.

About the Author

Erin McLellan is the author of several contemporary romances, all of which have characters who are complex, goodhearted, and a little quirky. She likes her stories to have a sexy spark and a happily ever after. Originally from Oklahoma, she currently lives in Alaska and spends her time dreaming up love stories set in the Great Plains. She is a lover of chocolate, college sports, antiquing, Dr Pepper, and binge-worthy TV shows. Erin is a member of Romance Writers of America and its Alaska chapter.